# DUSTY AYRES AND HIS BATTLE BIRDS:
## THE TROPOSPHERE F-S

# THE TROPOSPHERE
# F-S

*By Robert Sidney Bowen*

**ALTUS PRESS • 2019**

EDITED AND DESIGNED BY

Matthew Moring

ASSOCIATE EDITOR

Ray Riethmeier

PUBLISHING HISTORY

"The Troposphere F-S" originally appeared in the April, 1935 (Vol. 8, No. 1) issue of *Dusty Ayres and his Battle Birds* magazine. Copyright 2019 by Steeger Properties, LLC. All rights reserved.

# CHAPTER 1
## EKAR STRIKES

"**SWEETEST THING** with wings, she is now, skipper. You can serve notice on them Black Invader bums any old time you please!"

Dusty toed out his cigarette and grinned at the corporal mechanic.

"Thanks, Sweeney," he said. "I knew you'd put her in shape. One reason why I came down here to Pittsburgh Test Depot. You lads sure know your stuff. Here, split this with the other boys."

He tossed the man a ten dollar bill and started to leg into the cockpit of his X-Diesel pursuit. The corporal stopped him halfway.

"Couldn't think of it, skipper," he said. "Thanks, just the same."

"We'll gamble for it, corporal!" Dusty called from the pit, "The last figure of the serial number! Odd or even?"

"I'll guess odd!"

"Odd it is! You win! So long."

"It ain't skipper. Just looked—it's a six. It's—"

The rest of the mechanic's shout was lost in the roar of the X-Diesel as Dusty opened it up and practically leaped the ship into the air from a standing start.

Holding the nose heavenward, he climbed until twenty thousand feet of clear air were under his single wing. Then

leveling off, he shot forward at full throttle and glued his eyes
to the instrument panel.

"Not bad," he grunted. "Not bad at all. That long drink of water, Curly Brooks, will have to step to keep pace with papa now. And Biff, too. The bums—holding out that five bucks of mine last week. Damned if I don't think they split it between them. I'll hold the stakes myself, next time we have a race."

Easing the plane into a dive, he streaked earthward, then

pulled up in a long loop, double-rolled off the top, and let the ship whip-stall into a spin. Five thousand feet lower he pulled it out and set a dead-on compass course for the home drome of High Speed Group 7, just outside Springfield, Massachusetts.

A shade under thirty minutes later, he coasted down, touched rubber and taxied into the hangar line. As he opened up the orange peel glass cowl, slid out of his chute harness and legged-to the ground, the big, bulky figure of Biff Bolton came running up to him.

"Hey, skipper! Where'd you leave Curly?"

"Curly?" Dusty echoed. "What do you mean—where'd I leave him?"

Biff swallowed hard and his eyes widened.

"You—you mean to say—" he got out and then choked on the rest.

"Say what!" snapped Dusty. "For God's sake, Biff, get it off your chest!"

"That radio message you sent a couple of hours ago!" the big pilot exclaimed. "The one telling him to meet you at the old observation field outside Lowell. You said your ship was down, and for him to come in a cabin job to bring you back. Hell, he took Sergeant Pointon and some tools along with him!"

The words wouldn't come off Dusty's tongue for a couple of seconds. He simply stared at Bolton, as though he were staring at some kind of a freak, just dropped down from heaven. Then he grabbed him by the arm.

"Where's that radio message!" he yelled. "I don't know anything about it. Where is it, quick!"

"In Drake's—in the C.O.'s office!" the other blurted out.

Spinning on his heel, Dusty tore down the tarmac and barged in through the Group office door without even bothering to knock. Major Drake, seated in his chair behind the desk, jumped a foot.

"Hey! What the—oh, it's you, Ayres! Where's the fire?"

The pilot skidded across the floor, brought up sharp against the desk.

"That radio message!" he panted. "The one for Brooks! Where is it?"

Major Drake frowned, fixed him with a keen look.

"Wait a minute, Ayres! Keep your shirt on! What's all the—"

"Wait, hell!" Dusty broke in savagely. "I didn't send any message to Curly. Where is it? What's the wave-length recording number?"

The C.O.'s face paled under his wind bronze. He started to speak, then chopped it off, and grabbed a sheet of paper out of the tier of three boxes on the side of his desk.

"Here!" he said, bending over it. "This is the copy for my file. It was sent from Lowell area at two-twenty-two. Look at it yourself!"

Dusty was already looking at it over the C.O.'s shoulder.

Lieutenant Brooks

H.S.G. 7

Forced landing at old observation field near Lowell. Hop in a cabin ship and come get me.

(Signed) Ayres

"Radio Officer Clarkson received it, put it on paper, and brought it to me. I got in touch with Brooks and told him you wanted help. And you didn't send it, Ayres?"

Dusty hardly heard the CO. Face grim, brows furrowed, he gazed at the radiogram copy as little fingers of ice rippled up and down the small of his back.

"Huh?" he suddenly grunted. "No, of course I didn't send it! I came direct here from Pittsburgh. Damn it to hell!"

"Wait, Ayres! Where are you going?"

But the pilot was out the door and pounding dirt over to his plane. Biff Bolton shouted something at him, but he paid no attention. In a series of lightning-like movements, he leaped into his ship, booted the starter and sent the plane rocketing forward. Pulling it clear, he flattened out at an even hundred feet, and with throttle wide open, went hedge-hopping due north toward the city of Lowell.

STARTLED TROOPS and civilians gaped up as he hammered past. But he didn't even give them a look. Hunched motionless over the controls, he kept his eyes fixed rigidly ahead, and savagely cursed the plane on to greater speed.

In a matter of minutes, Lowell slipped by under his wings. He veered sharply toward the northwest outskirts of the city, cut across the Merrimac River, and went slanting down toward a barren and desolate triangular patch of ground two or three miles south of the New Hampshire border.

Seconds before his wheels touched, he saw the crumpled figure stretched out on the far side of the field. Sight of it made his heart go stone cold. He flung himself from the cockpit and ran the last twenty or thirty yards.

"Curly! Curly, old man! What have they—"

He choked off the rest as he reached the still figure and dropped to his knees. It was not Curly Brooks. It was Sergeant Pointon. He was dead—shot through the chest and head. The non-com's right hand was still stiffly grasping his half-drawn service automatic.

Dusty didn't touch him. There was nothing he could do. Sergeant Pointon had been dead for over an hour.

"Poor devil—poor devil! He was one of the best, too. God, if I ever get my hands on the rat who did it!"

He stood up, glanced about the field. There was nothing to see but the bordering trees. The hangars and buildings once there had long since been taken away. Only the field and the trees remained—with a dead man stretched out on the field.

Then, suddenly, the roar of an airplane engine snapped Dusty's eyes skyward, to the south. A tiny shadow was sweeping down toward the field. He took two running steps toward his plane and then stopped.

The shadow had become Biff Bolton's plane swinging down to a tail-up landing. The big pilot braked to a stop a dozen yards from him, leaped out and ran over. He didn't see the dead man until he had reached Dusty's side. Then he stiffened, stared hard.

"God, it's Pointon!" he rumbled.

"Shot twice!" Dusty explained. "Dead—and they've probably taken Curly with them."

"They?" Biff echoed. "Who? You saw them?"

7

"Hell no!" Dusty grated. "Think I'd be standing here if I had? No, I'm only guessing. They—sent that radio from here, probably from one of their ships that landed on this field. Curly came, and brought Pointon along. They weren't counting on Pointon—so they killed him, overpowered Curly, and took him off in the cabin job."

As Dusty talked he searched the broad expanse of cloud-dotted blue above his head, as though he expected suddenly to see a Black Invader ship go winging past. But if there were any Black ships up there, their pilots kept them well out of sight. Slowly, Dusty lowered his eyes, glanced at the dead man a moment, and then started over toward his plane.

"Nothing we can do here, Biff," he said heavily. "Better get back to the field. I'll radio Lowell Medical to come and get poor old Pointon. Married—three swell kids."

"Yeah!" rumbled Bolton. Then, "But we'll get him, skipper. We'll get Curly back, pronto!"

Dusty smiled at the grim, reckless determination stamped on Biff's face.

"You're damn right we will!" he grated. "Or kill every damn Black this side of hell. On second thought, I don't think they'll kill him yet."

Bolton's face brightened.

"God, I hope not!" he choked out. "But—but how come you think that?"

Dusty's smile faded as he gestured weakly.

"More guesswork," he said. "I've got a hunch that the rat is trying to smack at me through Curly. Yeah, and I've got another

8

hunch that I'll be hearing from him soon. Ten to one it'll be an invite for me to come and try to get Curly, after he's got the stage all set."

Dusty's voice sounded as though he were speaking his thoughts out loud to himself. Biff took hold of his arm, pulled him to a halt.

"Don't get you, skipper!" he said. "Him? Who's him?"

"One guess, Biff," grunted Dusty absently. "And you don't even need that."

The big pilot looked blank for a moment, then gulped out a curse.

"God!" he exclaimed. "You mean, Ekar, huh? Ekar, the Avenger?"

"No one else but!" Dusty replied grimly. "I've been wondering if that tramp died in England when we smashed up that nest of paralysis gas guns.

"The last I saw of him, he was sprawled out on the road as his car tipped over chasing Jack Horner and me. Right now, I'm pretty sure that Satan spared his life, and that he's back on this side of the Atlantic. Well, see you at the field."

"Wait a second, skipper," the other persisted. "If Ekar has got Curly, and he tells you where he is, say, up Canada way, you ain't gonna be fool enough to go—well, you know what I mean, run right into a trap, or something?"

Dusty balled his right fist, ground it into the palm of his other hand.

"Trap or no trap," he said in a deadly voice. "When I find out where Curly is, I'm going there and get him."

Before Bolton could say anything else, Dusty swung away from him, went over to his own ship, and legged in. A few seconds after that he was streaking up into the air, and contacting Lowell Medical Base on the radio. He got it on the first try.

"A dead air-force sergeant on the old flying field north of you!" he said bluntly, when the "go ahead" signal came through. "Please pick him up and send the body to H.S. Group Seven field for burial. This is Captain Ayres, of Seven, speaking. Check back, please!"

"Checking back now, Captain Ayres. Message received, okay. We will do as you ask immediately. Signing off."

The ear-phones made clicking sound, but the red signal light on the panel continued to blink. Dusty frowned at it, picked up the transmitter tube again.

"What's the matter, Lowell Medical?" he asked.

But it was not the voice of the radio operator at Lowell Medical Base that answered his question—not by a damn sight. It was a voice that was stamped on memory for life; a voice that he would recognize anywhere in the world.

In short, the voice of Ekar! Ekar, self-styled avenger of the death of the Invaders' great air ace, the Black Hawk.

"I have been waiting some time to get your wave-length signals, Captain Ayres. You took longer than I expected. I suppose you have found out by now, yes?"

DUSTY DIDN'T answer directly. Bending forward he peered hard at the station direction finder dial. The needle showed that the broadcast was being sent out by aircraft equipment from some point about three hundred- to three hundred-and-fifty miles northeast of his position.

"Did you hear me, captain? Are my signals coming through clearly? If not, let me know, and I will switch to a two-four-two reading. I have something important to tell you."

Two-four-two reading? Dusty's heart looped over as he heard that. Two-four-two was a private wave-length that he and Curly used when talking with each other while in flight. For a time it had been secret. But it was no longer secret—the Blacks had discovered it and used it to their own advantage some weeks ago. And now, ten to one, Ekar was mentioning it to make sure he'd not break the contact. Well, he wasn't going to anyway.

He pressed the transmitter tube to his lips.

"Your signals are clear enough on this length!" he grated. "Go ahead!"

"Excellent!" replied the ear-phones. "Now pay attention, Captain Ayres. Your friend, Lieutenant Brooks, is our prisoner. And if—"

"Listen, Ekar!" Dusty cut in savagely. "I'm making you a promise. If Brooks is hurt—if you do a single damn thing to him—I'll wring your neck!"

A rasping chuckle came out of the ear-phones.

"Am I to be frightened by that, captain? Listen, fool dog, it is useless for you to try to find your friend now. You can be of far more help to his, er—er welfare by doing absolutely nothing for the time being. You will hear again from me shortly. At that time you will receive unmistakable proof that Lieutenant Brooks is my prisoner, and instructions as to how you are to go about obtaining his return. You still hear me?"

Dusty swallowed hard, nodded as though the other stood in front of him.

"I hear you," he said. "But if you have any idea that I'm going to follow your instructions, you're crazy. Why, I'll—"

"I'm afraid you won't!" the voice in the ear-phones interrupted evenly. "The life of Lieutenant Brooks means nothing to me. But it means considerable to you, captain—more than you are perhaps willing to admit. And I intend to—"

The voice was cut off abruptly. A split second later there was the sound like the crack of a pistol and someone cried out in mortal pain. Then followed a hissing sound, the red light on the radio panel winked out, and the ear-phones went silent.

Dusty twisted on full volume, spun the wave-length dial needle. But it was all to no avail. He was unable to pick up the station again. Snapping off contact altogether, he coasted back toward the H.S. Group 7 drome, staring hopefully at the red signal light. It did not wink again.

Presently he slid down to a landing, taxied up to the line, and sat there in his ship, gazing narrow-eyed at nothing in particular. Biff Bolton roused him out of his bitter revery.

"Heard some of that, skipper!" the big pilot panted as he climbed up on the fuselage step and leaned in through the open cockpit cowling. "You were right. That mug's got Curly. Shall we slam up there and get him out?"

He stopped short as Dusty shook his head.

"No?" Biff echoed thickly. "Why not?"

Dusty didn't answer at once. He motioned Biff down off the step, legged out, and absently ran his hand along the sleek metal side of the ship.

"No use," he grunted as Bolton was about to repeat his question. "That broadcast was from a ship in the air. He wouldn't be fool enough to hang around in the same spot and wait for us to show up. God knows where he is now. But we've got to wait. He's playing his dirty game his way.

"Don't worry, if I thought we had a chance, I'd take off right now. But it would be simply flying in circles and maybe we'd do Curly more harm than good. That's the hell of it, don't you see? We've got to wait for the break, for Curly's sake."

Biff grimaced, ran a hand through his mop of shaggy hair.

"Yeah, it's hell right enough!" he rumbled. "We gotta think of Curly. You think maybe they haven't done nothing to him yet?"

"Your guess is as good as mine," Dusty replied, raising narrowed eyes toward the northern heavens. "I might be able to tell you if I knew how the hell they caught him. He was certainly expecting to see me there at that field. I can't understand why he landed. And—now what's this?"

A PLANE with Staff markings was sliding down onto the field. As soon as it touched it was quickly taxied up to the hangar line. It was a cabin job, and a major and two soldiers climbed out. The pilot remained in his seat. Saying something to the soldiers, that Dusty didn't catch, the major walked over to him, eyed him coldly.

"You are Captain Ayres, of course?" he snapped.

Dusty saluted.

"Yes sir," he said. "What can I do for you?"

The other gave him a withering look that started Dusty's blood heating up. Major or no major, he wasn't used to being regarded as something the cat had dragged in.

"You can come with me to your commanding officer!" the major cracked. "He's in his office, I suppose?"

With an effort, Dusty choked back a hot retort sliding up to his lips.

"He is, sir," he said quietly. "At least he was there a very short time ago. Nothing wrong, I hope?"

The senior officer motioned Dusty to start walking, and fell into step at his side. As they passed the staff plane, the two soldiers dropped in behind.

"Perhaps you didn't hear my question, sir," said Dusty as they approached the field office. "Is there something wrong?"

"There is, captain! And you will hear more about it when we get to New York!"

"New York? What—"

"Inside, captain! Ahead of me!"

The sharp command cut off the rest of Dusty's question. He hesitated a split second, flashed the senior officer a keen glance, and then without a word stepped through the field office door.

Major Drake, behind the desk, looked up as they entered, frowned, and got to his feet.

"What's all this about?" he grunted. "What brings you here, Saunders?"

The Staff major closed the door in the faces of the two guards, then walked over to Drake's desk, and handed him a folded paper.

"That will explain my visit, Major Drake!" he said importantly.

The C.O. gave him a hard look, unfolded the paper, and sucked in his breath sharply.

"My God, Saunders!" he shouted. "Has Staff gone crazy? What in hell's the idea? Why—why, on what grounds, what grounds?"

"That is not for me to say!" the Staff officer replied. "I am only carrying out the orders of General Babcock!"

Major Drake read whatever was on the paper again, cursed softly and snatched up the desk phone.

"Radiophone to General Babcock!" he barked into the mouthpiece. "Yes, he's at Northeastern Area H.Q., New York. Get me through at once. Yes, I'll hang on!"

There was a moment of silence, then Drake bent toward the mouthpiece again.

"Yes, yes! Oh, General Babcock? This is Major Drake, of High Speed—eh? Yes, he's here. That's what I'm— What? What? But I don't understand, why? What's the charge? Eh? But—yes sir. Very good, sir!"

He hung up, shoved the instrument away, and glared at the paper he still held in his hands. Presently he raised his eyes, looked at Dusty.

"Get your chin out, Ayres," he said heavily. "It's absurd, ridiculous—but General Staff orders, nevertheless. You are under arrest, and Major Saunders, here, is ordered to take you to Northeastern Area H.Q. for summary trial and indictment."

Dusty stood gaping at him, dumbfounded.

"Arrest?" he finally got out. "What the—I mean, arrest for what?"

Major Drake grimaced.

"General Babcock would not give me the details," he replied. "Simply said that it was for violation of section twenty-two of Military Rules and Regulations."

For a moment Dusty almost laughed out loud. He didn't though, simply swallowed hard.

"Why—why he's nuts!" he blurted out, in spite of the beady look Major Saunders gave him. "Section twenty-two is about the misuse of an officer's authority to the extent of causing serious loss and damage to allied commands. But, my God, I—!"

"I know!" the C.O. broke in, glaring at the staff major. "That's why this order is so damn ridiculous! I've half a mind not to turn Captain Ayres over to your charge."

Five seconds of electrified silence, and then the staff major motioned with his head at the closed door.

"You wish me to call in an armed guard and take him by force?" he snapped.

## CHAPTER 2
## INVISIBLE HELL

S LOUCHING BACK in the rear seat of the cabin plane, Dusty flicked a parting salute through the window at Major Drake as the motor roared up and the plane gathered speed. Then turning front, he fixed agate eyes on the back of the Staff major's head sitting in front of him. As though actually feeling the look, the officer turned and held out his hand.

"Your gun, please, captain!" he said sharply.

Dusty didn't know whether to hit him with it or not. He decided not, and handed it over without a word. By now the plane had cleared the ground and was swinging up and around to the south. Alone with his thoughts, Dusty fell to brooding over them and got madder by the second.

Of all the damn fool stunts that had ever been pulled, this took the fur-lined prop. Of course, there was some mistake, and everything would be cleared up eventually. But, in the meantime—Curly!

Ekar was going to get in touch with him later. When? Probably while he was trying to make a fatheaded bunch of staff officers realize they had pushed the wrong button.

Too bad he'd cooled the C.O. down and said he'd accompany Saunders to New York. Maybe it would have been better to have had a rip-snorting show-down right then and there. But, then again, no. There was a war still going on and personal items didn't matter a damn. Yeah! He'd get this dizzy thing over within nothing flat and get back to the task of getting Curly.

A sudden movement, forward in the cabin, jerked Dusty away from his rambling, bitter thoughts. The sergeant pilot, at the controls, was bending forward and staring up to the left.

"Something up there sir!" he called back to Major Saunders. "Can't see it very clearly. But I guess we'd better not take chances, and get down into the clouds."

Ignoring the soldier who sat rigidly beside him, Dusty leaned across his lap and squinted up out the side window. At first he saw nothing but cloud-dotted sky. And then, suddenly, he saw a moving oval-shaped blur.

It was too high to see anything in particular—just an oval-shaped shadow tearing past toward the south at terrific speed. Just a glimpse of it and the thing was gone. Or, rather, the sergeant pilot had sent them thundering down into an enveloping cloud bank and it was hidden from view.

"Pull her back up, sergeant!" Dusty called. "Let's take a good look at it. We can duck down again if we have to."

"Keep in the clouds, sergeant!" barked Major Saunders over his shoulder, as he spun on Dusty. "Head for New York, as fast as you can. And you, Captain Ayres, will please be quiet! You seem to forget that you are under arrest, and have absolutely no authority to give orders to anyone!"

Dusty caught himself in time, and grinned.

"Sorry, sir," he said quietly. "I was only thinking of our safety. Escorts for Black bombers usually fly in the clouds, or just under them. Just in case they meet unexpected enemy planes, you understand."

It was a swell lie, and it worked perfectly. Some of the forced military stiffness went out of Major Saunders. He went just a shade green under the eyes, and his hands gripped the sides of the seat tightly.

"An enemy bomber?" he managed to get out. "You saw it Captain Ayres?"

Dusty shrugged, forced a dubious look to his face.

"Not sure, sir," he said. "Maybe I could hide and seek us up through the clouds and make sure. But of course we can chance it, and carry on. There are chutes here for all of us."

And that was plenty for Staff Major Saunders. He gave Dusty a helpless, very much worried look, and turned to the pilot.

"Sergeant!" he ordered with as much dignity as he had left. "Let Captain Ayres take the controls. He's more experienced than you are. Captain! Find out if that's a bomber, and if it is, get us out of this damn mess!"

As Dusty exchanged seats with the sergeant pilot he thought he saw the non-com flash him a grin. He wasn't sure, but it served to make him believe that there was at least one other human being in the ship. The soldiers had acted like so much movable wood since the very beginning.

Hauling back the stick he sent the ship slamming up in a violent motion that spilled Saunders on the floor. The officer let out a bellow of fear that was a balm to Dusty's smouldering rage. The cardboard soldier would get more before the flight was over. But first, to get another look at that queer thing they'd seen.

Holding the nose up, Dusty cleared the cloud layer, climbed toward a second one, and went through it into clear air faintly tinged with the crimson glow of a dying sun. Swinging around so that the sun was at his back, he started to scan minutely the heavens on all three sides. To the north, and to the east he saw nothing. He twisted around to the south, and stiffened in the seat.

"My God! What the hell's them things—birds?"

Dusty hardly heard the sergeant pilot's sudden exclamation. He was staring fixedly at a spot of sky well over twenty miles ahead of him. Silhouetted against the crimson-tinged blue were three sun-haze-shrouded objects that looked like three prehistoric beetles with wings, sailing across the heavens in military airplane formation.

Every few seconds a shaft of sunlight caught them squarely and they glowed a blood-red. And then, without warning, all three of them went slanting down and became lost in the clouds.

"Captain! Captain! Are they enemy bombers? Are they—"

Dusty was trying desperately to slam his own ship down in a dive, but Major Saunders was half hanging over his shoulder. He jerked back his free elbow, and knocked the officer back into his seat.

"Back, damn you!" he roared. "Out of my way!"

THE MAJOR shouted something, but Dusty didn't stop to listen. The red signal light on the radio panel was blinking rapidly. He shot out his hand, snapped on contact, and spun the wave-length dial knob.

Nothing came out of the cabin speaker until he had turned the knob way below the lowest reading on the dial—as a matter of fact, turned it to a point exactly between the registered short-wave and longwave transmission bands. At that point the speaker unit gave forth a sound that was somewhat akin to the whir of an electric fan except that there was also a sharp electric crackle in the sound. The volume was constant and the sound neither decreased nor increased even though Dusty's ship was changing altitude rapidly.

"Know what that is, skipper?" the sergeant pilot's voice came to Dusty's ear.

He shook his head.

"No, do you?"

"Maybe," was the reply. "Heard something like it once before—by accident. It was at Dayton test field about six months ago. They were trying out some electrically-driven propellers for small coastal motorboats. I happened to be fooling with the wave-band detector machine in the radio hut. Well, I picked up the stuff they were testing, and it sounded just like that."

"You mean you picked up the motor disturbance?" Dusty shot at him.

"Yeah—oh sure, not the props, of course!"

Dusty looked hard at the cabin speaking unit, out of which the strange noise was still pouring.

"Hell, I wonder!" he breathed. Then, "No, that's out absolutely. Too much weight!"

"Huh, skipper?" said the non-com. "What are you saying?"

"Forget it," Dusty shrugged. "I was wondering if those cock-eyed things we're trying to tag are run by electric motors. But they couldn't carry the weight. Besides, we only picked up this dizzy noise right after they went into the dive. And—"

THE MAN GAVE A WEIRD GURGLING CRY.

22

He didn't finish. At that instant the speaker unit gave out a sharp click, and went silent. And a moment later the plane raced down through the last of the clouds and out into clear air. A quick glance at the ground below told Dusty that they were over the Connecticut-New York line.

Leveling off he peered hard to the south, but the fading light transformed ground and clouded sky into one great limitless blur. There wasn't a single sign of the strange objects they had seen above the clouds.

Easing back the throttle to the three-quarter mark, he started to drift about in a series of wide circles when Major Saunders leaned over and touched him on the shoulder.

"Never mind hanging around here, captain!" he snapped. "Get on to New York, with all speed possible. You can land us on the Central Park field. We're to be met there by car."

Dusty nodded absently, his eyes still fixed on the southern horizon. But a few seconds later he whirled into lightning-like action. From above and behind came the savage yammer of aerial machine-gun fire, and steel hammers beat against the fuselage cabin roof.

"My God! What's that?" came Major Saunders' wild cry. "We're being attacked. Captain—"

"Shut up, and hang on!" Dusty bellowed.

And with that he hurled the craft over on wingtip and spun around in a split-arc turn. The hammering on the cabin roof changed to the side, and in the next split second the right cabin window melted into oblivion and unseen wasps whined through and smacked against the flooring.

23

They passed so close to Dusty that he almost believed he felt their heat against the back of his neck. Behind him, one of the soldiers let out a weird gurgling cry, clutched at his throat, and went sprawling off his chair.

"Oh my God—he's been hit! He's dead!"

The staff major's wailing sounds were but faint echoes in Dusty's ears. Working the controls furiously, he was concentrating on swinging the plane around and up so as to get a look at the sudden attacker. But though he searched every square foot of sky and clouds about him, he saw nothing—not even the tell-tale stream of jetting flame zipping down.

By now the mysterious firing had stopped. Dusty, however, was too much of a veteran to consider that fact as a sign that his unseen foe had drifted off to other parts. Thumbs against the electric trigger-trips ready to jab forward instantly, he prop-clawed upward toward the protecting clouds.

To fly underneath them, in clear air, was but to ask for a stomach full of singing steel. The staff plane was fast, as planes go, but with its present load aboard it was no match for an enemy pursuit job. And an enemy pursuit the unknown ship must have been, even though he had not sighted it.

The very fact that it had faded out of sight before he could swing around and up, was proof positive of that fact. Therefore, the clouds were their best bet.

Forty seconds of nerve-tingling suspense, and then the prop chewed into the fringy bottom of the clouds, clawed into them and pulled the plane in after it. Hidden once more, Dusty swung south, leaned forward and kept his eyes glued to the instrument board.

A hard smile curled his lips. Wasn't this the damnedest ever? A man under arrest was doing his utmost to bring himself to trial safely! It was certainly one for the book, and no mistake about it.

FOR A full half hour he plunged dead south in the enveloping clouds. Out the tail of his eye he saw Major Saunders getting more nervous and perplexed with each passing minute. A dozen times the Staff officer started to lean forward, as though to tap Dusty on the shoulder, but each time he checked the movement and slumped back in his seat.

"If the thing wasn't so damn serious," Dusty grunted softly to himself, "damned if I don't believe I'd fly that bum out to sea and force-land, just for the hell of it!"

"What were you saying just then, captain?" came Saunders' sharp voice. "Something's happened?"

"Just wondering about our chances of reaching New York, sir," Dusty answered easily. "Guess I'll get out of these clouds now. Keep your eyes open, everyone."

Shoving the stick forward, he sent the plane sliding down into clear air once more. That is, clear air darkening with approaching twilight.

The ground was just a murky blur, dotted here and there by clusters of lights. By checking with them and the roller map fitted to the instrument panel, Dusty placed his position as being about one hundred miles due south of New York. To be exact, at the northern entrance of Delaware Bay.

Cutting around, he headed back toward New York at full throttle. And it was then that the red signal light on the radio panel started blinking. A quick glance at the dial showed that some station was sending out signals on an S.O.S. Emergency wave-length reading.

Realization set his blood to dancing, and in one sweeping movement of his free hand he snapped on contact and spun the wave-length dial knob to the true reading. Instantly the cabin speaker unit crackled out sound.

"… assistance at once! Send air assistance at once. Bombers have destroyed munition factories. Area in flames now. Unable to check them. Could not sight enemy bombing planes. Please contact Coastal Patrol. Transmitter going out—can no longer send signals. Send assistance to V Twenty-four at once please. Send—"

The rest died out in fuzzy sound, and finally the speaker unit went silent. Turning on full reception volume did not even raise a whisper. The broadcasting station had gone off the air for good.

"V Twenty-four? Where's V Twenty-four, captain?"

Dusty didn't answer Major Saunders' shouted question immediately. In fact he didn't even turn until he was convinced that there was no hope of picking up any more signals. And then, he addressed his remark to the sergeant pilot at his side.

"V Twenty-four is the navy munitions base at Newport News," he grunted. "Hell, our coastal planes must be all in their hangars. How the devil could enemy bombers get over V Twenty-four without being spotted in time?"

The non-com shrugged, furrowed his brows and looked straight at Dusty.

"Maybe I'm nuts, skipper," he said slowly, "but I'm just wondering if it was bombs. Newport News is on the water, or near enough, and—"

He stopped as though reluctant to state the rest of his views. Dusty nodded.

"Yeah, maybe you're right, sergeant," he said. "You were going to say that Black ships off shore could shell it?"

"Something like that," the other replied. "But we've got ships of our own standing off shore. Can't see how they'd just sit back and let the Blacks poke stuff over their heads."

Major Saunders, who had been leaning forward listening intently, suddenly broke into the conversation.

"Well, it's no affair of ours!" he snapped tartly. "The bombers have obviously gone, and we can't keep General Staff waiting any longer!"

The officer's words jerked Dusty's thoughts back to the real reason why he was in the plane. In the excitement of the last several minutes he had forgotten all about that. He started to speak, but checked himself and nodded grimly.

"Yes sir," he grunted. "I'm coasting in now. New York is dead ahead."

By way of confirming his words he eased back the throttle and allowed the plane to slide down toward the southern tip of Manhattan Island. Not since the time when the Black Invaders had tried to destroy New York, many months ago, had he flown over the great city. And now as he glided toward it he studied it intently. The lower half was more or less in ruins, as was a large section of old Brooklyn. The upper half, however, was still very much intact; spared by some miracle, the results of that terrific but fruitless onslaught of some time ago.

Sliding down over the inner harbor, he fed a bit of hop to the engine, thundered over the war-smashed area, and finally coasted down to a perfect landing on the flood-lighted landing field in Central Park. The instant he had taxied up to the administration building and cut the switch, Major Saunders, his courage and military dignity regained, immediately took charge.

He climbed down quickly from the plane, turned and pointed back at the dead soldier on the floor of the cabin and nodded at the non-com pilot.

"You will take charge of him, sergeant!" he barked. "I suggest that you contact the medical unit, here at the field. And you, Captain Ayres, will get out of the plane and accompany me. And you," to the other soldier, "will follow us two paces to the rear."

All that off his chest, the man stepped back and waited for his orders to be obeyed. Holding back the hot words on his lips, Dusty started to climb out of the seat. As he did, the non-com pilot leaned close to him.

"Don't know what it's all about, skipper," he said in a low voice, "but a million in luck, anyway. It was a swell ride!"

Dusty grinned, gave him a pat on the arm.

"Thanks, buzzard," he said. "I don't know what it's all about, myself. By the way, what's your name?"

"Coggins," the sergeant replied. "Attached to Staff Air Transport—and is it lousy work!"

Dusty was out of the plane now and unable to answer as Saunders was closing in on him like some village gossip anxious to hear every single word. So he didn't say anything. Simply nodded and made a mental note to remember the name of Sergeant Coggins. Like Biff Bolton had once been, Coggins was not where he could do the most good for his country. Maybe he could do something about that sometime.

"This way, captain! Hurry, please!"

DUSTY TURNED, dropped into step with the Staff officer and walked down the front of the administration building toward a waiting car. As they approached, the driver behind the wheel leaped out, opened the rear door and stood rigidly at attention.

Saunders, beaming, gave him a stiff nod, climbed in back and motioned Dusty in at his side. The soldier got into the front seat, the driver took his place behind the wheel, and the car rolled forward.

"By the way, Captain Ayres," Saunders spoke up suddenly. "Your language to me in front of those enlisted men was not what it should have been. You understand?"

Dusty gave him an agate look.

"Nor was your courage in the face of danger," he grated. "You understand that?"

The other's face went beet-red, and for a moment Dusty thought that his tailor-made escort was going to throw a fit.

He got control of himself somehow, and bored Dusty with his fishy blue eyes.

"And I shall add insubordination to the other charges!" he snapped.

Dusty got it out before he could stop himself.

"And some day I'm going to take you apart, and see what makes you tick!"

That was the last straw. Saunders, acting as though he had Fire-Eyes himself under his charge, whipped his automatic from its holster and held it against Dusty.

"One move, Captain Ayres!" he bellowed, "and I shall shoot—I promise you!"

Dusty looked from the gun up into the other's face.

"No," he said in an even voice, "I won't take you apart. I'll just smack you one and let you fall apart!"

Whatever the enraged Staff officer was going to do next, was halted in the bud, for at that moment the car slid to a stop in front of the Northeastern Area Staff building—formerly the famous 71st Regiment armory.

Still holding the gun on Dusty as the soldier and the driver stood gaping pop-eyed on the sidewalk, Saunders ordered him out, and herded him inside the building. There they met the guard officer, who spoke in low tones with Saunders, and then led them up to the second floor of the building to offices at the rear. A sharp knock on the door brought a gruff summons from within. The guard officer opened the door and stood to one side.

Major Saunders, gun holstered by now, straightened up so stiffly that his neck must have hurt.

"Prisoner Captain Ayres—forward march!"

## CHAPTER 3
## THE DOOMED FLOTILLA

S EETHING WITH raging anger inside, but outwardly steady and calm, Dusty marched into the room, clicked his heels and snapped a smart salute at the group of over-stuffed, gold-braided figures seated about a table in the center of the room. A few of them, he recognized, but neither General Horner nor General Bradley, Chief of Air Force Staff was among them. As a matter of fact, the majority were high-ranking navy men. The minority, War Department officials.

As Dusty saluted, a gimlet-eyed admiral at the far end of the table stood up and nodded.

"Thank you, Major Saunders!" he boomed. "That is all. Dismissed. Captain Ayres! Advance to the table please!"

Dusty walked forward until he was a pace or so from the table. The ring of officers fixed him with half frowning eyes. Then the admiral spoke again.

"Captain Ayres! You will please explain to this summary trial court the reason for your stupid and costly action of yesterday—during the late afternoon, to be exact!"

Dusty blinked and swept the group with his eyes.

"I'm afraid I do not understand, sir," he said quietly. "What action of mine are you referring to?"

The admiral made a grunting noise in his throat, pursed his lips, and glared at Dusty.

"It is highly advisable that you give us a complete account, captain!" he thundered. "This court has proof of what you did. Trying to evade the issue will only go hard with you."

Dusty battled for control, but didn't do a very good job of it.

"You may know what you are talking about, sir!" he snapped. "But I certainly don't. Ever since that—since Major Saunders arrived at my field with General Babcock's arrest order, I have been wondering what in—what it was all about. I assure you, sir, I haven't the faintest idea!"

A low, disgruntled sort of murmur ran from lip to lip. The admiral coughed, tapped his fingers on the edge of the table. "Did you not, while on solo patrol yesterday afternoon," he suddenly began, "sight enemy submarines off the New Jersey coast?"

"Why no, sir," Dusty replied instantly.

The admiral seemed to ignore his answer.

"And did you not send an S.O.S. Emergency, with your own A-Six code signal, for the Fourth Destroyer flotilla to go out in search of those submarines?"

"Send a—"

Dusty stopped, swallowed hard, stared at the other as though unable to believe his ears.

"Send an S.O.S. Emergency?" he repeated. "Sighted enemy submarines? Hell, no! Of course not! As a matter of fact I wasn't anywhere near the New Jersey coast yesterday. My plane wasn't acting right, and I spent most of yesterday afternoon checking on it!"

The ring of officers about the table arched their eyebrows.

"And you can, of course, prove where you were all that time?" the officiating admiral shot at him.

"Why, of—"

Dusty killed the rest and cursed inwardly. Proving where he had been all yesterday afternoon was one thing he couldn't do. He'd been alone all of the time, mostly at high altitude. The feed jet of the X-Diesel had acted up, and he'd spent most of the time trying to adjust it. He hadn't succeeded, and as a result had flown down to Pittsburgh Test that very morning. No, he couldn't prove a thing about yesterday afternoon.

He steeled himself, looked the admiral straight in the eye.

"No sir," he said. "I cannot prove where I was all during yesterday afternoon. I can only say that I was in the air, and ask you to accept my word that I was no where near the New Jersey coast, and know nothing about any enemy submarines being sighted off the coast."

The admiral shrugged.

"Knowing your record, Captain Ayres," he said solemnly, "this trial court certainly wants to accept your word. But it so happens that we have proof that you did sight the enemy submarines, and used the special authority invested in you by the President and the Congressional Committee, to the extent of ordering the Fourth Flotilla out after them."

IT WAS all that Dusty could do to stop from telling them all the thoughts uppermost in his mind at that moment. He felt as though he were in the midst of a cockeyed nightmare, and that the naval stuffed-shirts about the table were nocturnal imps hurling crazy accusations at him.

"You have proof, sir?" he finally blurted out. "May I ask what that proof is?"

EKAR

The admiral nodded. "Certainly."

Reaching out his hand, the ranking officer jabbed a bell button on the desk. A side door instantly opened, and an infantry captain walked into the room and saluted smartly. The admiral returned the salute with a nod, pointed a finger at Dusty.

"Captain Wicks," he said, "do you know that officer?"

Gray eyes swept across Dusty's face.

"Yes sir! He is Captain Ayres of the air force, sir."

"Have you ever seen him before, Captain Wicks?"

"Yes sir, several times."

BIFF BOLTON

"And the last time you saw him?"

"Yesterday evening, sir. Shortly before six o'clock!"

Dusty's blood began to burn through his veins. The infantry officer was a total stranger to him.

"You talked to him, did you not, Captain Wicks?" asked the admiral.

"Yes sir. I was having a cocktail at the Army-Navy Club. Captain Ayres was there, too. I recognized him of course. Asked him what he was doing in New York. You see—"

"Get to the point, Captain Wicks!" the admiral barked. "What was Captain Ayres' reply?"

"He said that he was on the way back to his own drome, at Springfield, sir."

"And what else?"

"Why he said that he'd sighted some enemy submarines off the Jersey coast and added that our destroyers had probably settled their hash by now. He regretted that he couldn't take the time to check, but had to get back to his field. Right after that, he left."

"You rat! You know damn well you're lying! You never talked with me yesterday or at any other time!"

The raging words poured off Dusty's lips like water going over a broken dam. He would have leaped at the man, only two of the officers at the table jumped up and grabbed him and held him fast.

"Silence, Captain Ayres! Silence, do you hear me?"

The admiral punctuated his booming words by banging his clenched fists on the table. Dusty, trembling with anger, slowly relaxed, then stiffened to attention.

"I beg your pardon, sir," he said. "Captain Wicks, however, is lying. I have not been in the Army-Navy Club here in New York since the war started."

Tingling silence settled over the room for a moment. Presently the admiral nodded at the infantry captain.

"That is all, Captain Wicks," he said, "You are dismissed, but hold yourself prepared to give your testimony again, if called upon."

The infantry officer saluted smartly, flashed Dusty a half puzzled, half angry look, did a snappy about-face and marched out of the room.

As the door closed behind him, the admiral bent his eyes on Dusty again.

"There is our proof, Captain Ayres," he said tersely. Incidentally, there are others who saw you drinking a cocktail at the Army-Navy Club. Now, I suggest that you stop trying to cover yourself up, and explain the whole affair.

"The charge against you is serious—all the more serious because your action yesterday was in direct contrast to your past record. Your record, however, must be overlooked in the face of existing circumstances. Now, why did you send the Fourth Flotilla to its doom?

"Why did you not even accompany them to the spot where you sighted the submarines? And why did you not give the commander the correct position of the enemy underwater craft?"

**DUSTY SWAYED** unsteadily on his feet, raised his hand and brushed it across his eyes as though trying to remove the scene in front of him. But when he looked again it was still there. A ring of beetle-browed Staff officers glaringly waiting for his words. He tried to talk, but somehow the words just wouldn't come out. Finally, with a tremendous effort he got them off his stiffened lips.

"There is nothing that I can explain, gentlemen," he addressed them all. "I deny all the charges, and repeat that I know absolutely nothing about them."

The admiral's face darkened with anger.

"Let me remind you, captain, that this is but a summary trial," he said. "You can expect no favor whatsoever from a general court martial. For the last time, I am giving you an opportunity to advance some sort of a defense of your almost unbelievable miscarriage of authority."

Dusty hesitated, clenched his fists.

"May I be permitted to ask this court two questions?"

They all nodded affirmatively.

"You may," said the admiral.

Leaning forward, Dusty fixed his eyes on the face of the officiating officer.

"Did any of the destroyer flotilla get back?" he asked in a tense voice.

"Not a single ship!" replied the admiral harshly. "All six of the flotilla were sunk without trace. But before the commander's ship went down he radioed Navy H.Q. that they had been covered by a gas screen, and destroyed by torpedoes before they could defend themselves. It was then that we learned from Commander Stebbins, that you had sent them the S.O.S. order while on patrol! Your next question?"

Dusty started to shrug with hopeless resignation, then straightened up grimly.

"Did anyone in the flotilla see my plane?" he asked. "And if no one did, where was I supposed to have left my plane while I went to the Army-Navy Club for a cocktail?"

The stuffed-shirts glanced questioningly at each other, and the admiral chewed his lip in silent thought for a moment. Presently he half shook his head and arched his shaggy eyebrows.

"There was no report that the flotilla sighted your plane," he said. "Nor any report of where you landed before proceeding to the Army-Navy Club. The various fields about the city will have to be checked for accurate information. That can be done without any trouble."

"Then I suggest that you do it at once, sir!" Dusty clipped at him. "And I might add that you'll meet with considerable trouble. The reason being that I wasn't within shooting distance of any New York field yesterday, or the day before, or the week before. And what's more, I demand the right to see General Bradley and General Horner!"

The admiral went through his little trick act of pursing his lips, and furrowing his brows. Then he said,

"You will have to wait, captain! Neither General Horner nor General Bradley is in this area at the moment. Nor do I believe they are at Washington. However, it is your right to see them, and you will, before the date set for your court martial."

It was then that the final truth crashed home to Dusty. Unconsciously he went back a step.

"You mean?" he gasped incredulously. "You mean that I am to be detained, to be held for court martial—removed from active duty?"

The other nodded vigorously.

"Of course you are to be removed from active duty!" he said sternly. "Frankly, I am surprised at your attitude, captain. I had hoped for some plausible explanation of yesterday's incident. Yes, even hoped that we might be able to dismiss the charges against you.

"But, well, you seem desirous of taking a diametrically opposite course. So, by military law, I am forced to hold you for further trial and examination. Such an announcement will go out in general orders tonight—after I have submitted the findings of this court to General Babcock!"

And then Dusty went haywire. He leaped forward, pounded the table with his fist and shook the other hand at the admiral.

"For the love of God, listen to reason!" he roared. "You can't hold me, do you hear? You can't. I have something to do that may mean life or death. To hell with your findings—it's all a pack of lies—nothing but lies. I didn't see any enemy submarines! I didn't send any S.O.S. call to any destroyer flotilla! And I haven't been within fifty miles of New York in the last three weeks. My God, can't you get that through your heads?"

He would have said plenty more, only the admiral had jabbed the button on the table, and two armed guards had rushed in and seized him. The instant they grabbed him, he relaxed, and stood looking beseechingly at the ring of bewhiskered faces about the table.

"Take the prisoner to the detention cells, and put a guard over him!" the admiral thundered. "By God, I never believed I'd live to hear a young pup say—"

Words failed him. He made an angry dismissal gesture and sat down.

Thoughts spinning in mad, blood-red circles, Dusty allowed the two guards to lead him out the side door and down a corridor to the elevators. His movements were mechanical. He felt like a knocked-out boxer being led back to his dressing room. He hardly knew he was moving. Completely dazed, sick at heart, yet seething with rage, he blindly stumbled along, a guard holding him by each arm.

# CHAPTER 4
# THE DOUBLE EAGLE

A DULL clanging sound eventually penetrated Dusty's senses and caused him to look up. It was then that he realized he was behind the bars of a detention cell, and that one of the guards was closing the door and twisting the key in the lock. The other guard had disappeared.

Swaying slightly on his feet Dusty absently fished in his pockets for a cigarette, found none and stumbled over to the barred door.

"Got a smoke, soldier?" he muttered.

The guard gave him a sympathetic smile.

"Sorry, sir," he said, "but it's against regulations. I'd like to—I've heard about you, sir—but they'd have my hide. And, well, you know how it is."

Dusty nodded vacantly.

"Yeah," he murmured heavily. "I know how it is. Thanks just the same."

Turning slowly, he walked over to the bunk that lined the rear wall, sat down and rested his head in his hands. He tried to think but couldn't. Eventually, when thoughts began to rush upon him in a wild jumble, he tried to drive them away.

That it would work out all right, he realized deep down inside. A mysterious, horrible mistake had been made. The infantry captain—God knows why—had told a rotten lie. So, for that matter, had the dead commander of the destroyer flotilla.

No, that was a hell of a thing to say of a dead man. Yet, why had the man said that he had sent the S.O.S. Emergency call? He had never contacted the Fourth Flotilla in his whole life, and General Army-Navy Staff was actually believing the impossible. Not unusual, of course! General Staff was that way lots of times. It never seemed to be in the cards for Staff to be any different.

Oh the hell with trying to figure it out. The point at stake was Curly's welfare! Had Ekar tried to contact him again? Where was Curly? Was this the reward of a man who tried to do his best—was willing to sacrifice his life—everything for his country's cause? Was he just to be another political football for Staff to boot around until the real truth came out?

He didn't even try to answer the questions. Gradually he ceased thinking. Time became one dull, meaningless moment following the last one into eternity. When the cell door opened and food was brought in by the guards, he simply stared at it, and made no effort to eat. The guard said something to him, but he didn't hear what it was; made no effort to find out.

And so the time dragged on. The light of day, coming through the small barred window at the top of the rear wall, slowly faded into early twilight. And then—it seemed a lifetime to Dusty— the guard opened the door and ushered a second figure inside. At first Dusty took no notice of him. But suddenly, as he gave the newcomer a steely, defiant look, he jerked up to his feet with a rasping gasp.

The newcomer was Jack Horner.

"Jack! Jack!" Dusty shouted hoarsely, grabbing him by both arms. "My God, kid, everything's gone—"

"Hold it!" the Intelligence man cut him off sharply, twisting himself loose. "Follow me and be quiet!"

Ignoring Dusty, he turned to the guard and nodded.

"All right!" he snapped. "You have my signature for the prisoner. I'll be responsible for him. Come along, Ayres!"

It was not until they were outside and rolling away in a car that Agent 10 gave any attention to Dusty. Guiding the car through military and civilian traffic, he turned his head and regarded his friend gravely.

"How in hell did you get into such a mess, Dusty?" he asked. "When I heard about you and that flotilla act, I thought I was hearing things."

Dusty faced him angrily.

"Listen, Jack!" he grated, "not you too, for God's sake! I give you my solemn word that I didn't have a damn thing to do with it!"

"I believe you, kid," the other grinned. "Hell, do you think I'd be here if I didn't?"

"Just what I've been wanting to ask you," Dusty said. "How the hell did you get me out? And why?"

"The answer to the first," replied young Horner, "is because of special consideration granted the Intelligence department. It so happens that we are permitted to take any prisoner, one of our own men, or one of the enemy, under custody.

"I read about you in General Orders a little over an hour ago. I hot-footed it down here, exercised my special privilege as an officer in the department, and here you are. Hell, they'd never have done that if the general or Bradley had been there. Between you and me, Babcock and a few navy men are due for the axe, and assignment to some spot where they won't get into people's way."

And I'd love to be their escort!" grated Dusty. "But, listen, Jack, I don't want you to go getting your neck—"

"Let me worry about my neck," the other cut him off. "There's lots of other things more important just now."

"My God, yes!" Dusty exclaimed. "Listen, Jack, Ekar has got Curly! He got him this morning and—"

He stopped abruptly and stared at Jack Horner who was nodding his head.

"You know?" he gasped. "You know about Curly?"

"I know that Ekar has him," the Intelligence man said. "Found out just before I came down for you. Know how it happened? What are the details?"

His words running over one another, Dusty told him all he knew.

"And the rat's to contact me again!" he finished up. "And when those lugs arrested me, brought me here to New York, and—oh well, skip it! But how in hell did you find out about Curly? Did Ekar—"

"No! I saw Ekar and Curly in the C-Ray focusing plate."

Had the car looped the loop at that moment, Dusty wouldn't have even noticed. The C-Ray focusing plate! Instantly his mind rushed back to the time several days ago when the C-Ray had more or less saved his life, to say nothing of the lives of Curly, Biff, and Jack Horner.

THE C-RAY, so called because its inventor was a scientist by the name of Cook, was an instrument that could reproduce upon a special frosted glass screen a moving picture of any selected spot within a range of fifteen hundred miles. It was composed of two distinct and separate parts. The first was a small flashlight-appearing object that was known as the C-Ray recording cell. It could be carried about in the pocket, and placed anywhere. Its lens, of secret manufacture, trapped all light waves passing before it, and transmitted them back in the form of light wave vibrations to the second part of the instrument, known as the C-Ray focusing plate.

The power of the cell, or cells, was constant. But the focusing plate could be adjusted to any amount of light-wave power.

Thus when the light-wave picture, trapped by the lens of the C-Ray cell, was reproduced on the focusing plate and was blurred and indistinct, sufficient focusing power could be applied to make the picture clear.

Not only was the instrument for use on the ground, and in multiple form, but a single focusing plate for airplane use had been developed as well. The airplane unit was the one Dusty had used to good advantage. And now the C-Ray, of all things, had proved that Curly was still alive!

"C-Ray?" he gulped at his pal. "How the devil did you get—"

"Tell you all about it soon!" shouted Agent 10, pressing down on the car's siren button. "Hang on! I'm going to let this thing out!"

And that was exactly what the Intelligence man did. Feeding maximum hop to the high-powered engine under the hood, he sent the car thundering through the outskirts of New York, swung onto the wide Seaboard Boulevard, and went tearing along the shore toward the Connecticut line.

Dusty made no attempt at asking further questions. The roaring whine of the motor would have muffled his loudest shout. So he simply sat tight and waited for Agent 10 to get them to wherever they were headed.

Fifteen minutes more of road burning proved the place to be an old deserted country estate, four or five miles north of the city of Stamford. Swinging off the main road young Horner drove past the main house and pulled up in front of the garage a hundred yards in back.

No sooner had he stopped, than the car was surrounded by a ring of shabbily dressed farm workers. Each of them carried a machine gun, and the muzzle of each machine gun was trained on them.

Dusty saw all that in the reflected glow of the headlights. Then he heard Agent 10's low voice. Just one word.

"Duluth!"

Immediately the guns were lowered, and a figure approached the side of the car where Agent 10 sat. A flashlight snapped into life, sprayed a light on the Intelligence man's face, and then winked out.

"Okay, sir," said the owner of the light.

"Had us worried for a moment. You came up pretty fast."

"Guess I did at that," grunted Jack Horner, climbing out. "Come along, Dusty."

Complying with the request, Dusty followed his pal around in back of the garage and in through the rear door. Inside was like any civilian garage, but he didn't have time to notice anything in detail.

Young Horner steered him through a side door, and down a short flight of steps to another door. On this door the Intelligence man knocked four times, waited a few seconds, and then gave the door panel three quick raps.

It opened immediately and the muzzle of another machine gun confronted them, held by another shabbily dressed civilian. He lowered it, however, after scrutinizing them both, and stepped back.

Jack Horner immediately pushed Dusty ahead into a small, low-ceilinged room. It was like an electrical laboratory. Better still, it was like a high-powered broadcasting control room.

47

Both sidewalls were fitted up with numerous instrument panels. And on benches lining them were transmitter and radio receiving units.

The rear wall was also covered with instruments, but in the center was one that Dusty recognized instantly. It was a C-Ray cell focusing plate. In front of it, and a bit to one side, a man sat bent over an inclined table panel.

He didn't even look up as Dusty and Agent 10 entered. There was a scowl on his face, and his lips twitched angrily as he fingered a row of rheostats and small throw-switches on the right hand edge of the panel.

Brushing past Dusty, young Horner went over to him.

"What the hell happened, Carter?" he snapped. "Don't tell me that—"

He cut off the rest as the man looked up and shook his head.

"Don't know what the hell happened, lieutenant!" the man said bitterly. "It was clear as could be. The three of them were there, and then *blooey*—something went haywire, and the whole damn thing faded out. I'm still trying to get it back—but no soap, so far!"

Jack Horner smothered a curse, pointed at the row of rheostats.

"How about the others?" he grunted. "Anything showed up on them?"

"No, not a thing! I wonder if they caught Travis? He got this one right on schedule. And I can't understand why he didn't place the others, unless—God, I don't want to even think of it. Travis was my buddy!"

The man ended it with a low groan, and bent over the table panel again. Agent 10 watched him for a moment, then turned and motioned Dusty over to the side wall.

"Travis one of your men?" asked Dusty before Agent 10 said anything.

The Intelligence man nodded.

"Yeah, and a good one. Listen, kid, don't interrupt. I'll give you the whole story—as much as I know anyway."

He stopped long enough to scowl over at the C-Ray focusing plate, then returned his gaze to Dusty's face.

"YOU'LL REMEMBER," he began, "that before we started that St. Alabans, England, show, a couple of weeks ago, that my father said he expected the Blacks to try something new, darn soon.

"When you and I, and Biff and Curly, found out about their intention of bombarding us from England with long range paralysis gas guns, we thought that that was to be the big stunt. Maybe it was, but it wasn't all.

"There is still something damn screwy about the Blacks' movements up north of the Canadian front. Now the reports that have been coming through from our agents up there, haven't made it possible for us to put our finger on a single damn thing.

"All we've been able to find out, definitely I mean, is that Fire-Eyes has moved his H.Q. to Bersimis, a small town on the west bank of the St. Lawrence. That we do know."

The Intelligence man paused long enough to wet his lips, then continued.

"Now, here's the point. Since the destruction of their Shoal

Harbor naval base, the Blacks have made Bersimis their main naval base on the northern continent. And from what little we've been able to find out, Bersimis has also become their main North American air depot. The answer we want is this—why all this concentration at Bersimis?

"Are they planning to co-ordinate everything in one crashing attack against us? Or have our armies so weakened their lines that they are making arrangements to fall back to Bersimis and dig in for the Winter, and slam out harder than ever with the coming of Spring?"

"Damned if I know!" grunted Dusty as young Horner hesitated. "If they are, now is the time for us to knock them dizzy. But, listen, skip that for a second—tell me about Curly. Is he up there at Bersimis?"

"He is, or was an hour ago," Agent 10 nodded. "But hold your horses. In order to check on the meager reports that came through from our agents, we supplied them with some of the C-Ray cells—dropped them at night by chute. A young pilot named Stafford did the job. That was three days ago.

"The kid never came back. At least he hasn't come back yet. We don't know what happened to him. Didn't even hear anything by air. But he did drop some of the cells, and our man, Travis, got hold of them.

"Whether any of the other agents did, we don't know yet. For three days and nights we've been here, waiting for word, hoping against hope.

"Shortly after noon today, we got a recording on the plate, of one of the cells. It showed a room, an office, I guess. Some

Black colonel was seated at the desk. He worked on some papers, and then went out of the picture.

"For the next four hours nothing happened in the room. And then, none other than Fire-Eyes himself came in! God, to see him and not be able to do anything damn near sent me nuts. Soon after that, Ekar appeared in the picture. And then—I saw Curly. They'd mussed him up, but he was conscious, and able to walk, they—"

"The rats! The dirty rats!"

As Dusty growled the words he locked his fingers and squeezed his palms together as though crushing something to a pulp.

"Shut up, I'm talking!" snapped Agent 10. "They didn't do anything to him there. Seemed to be shooting questions at him, from the way he shook his head. Shortly after that I read about you in a radio copy of general orders. I got an idea, and went down after you."

Agent 10 paused, scowled at the floor as though choosing the words to say next. Dusty waited several seconds, then reached out and tapped him on the arm.

"Shoot, kid!" he grunted. "Let's have it. What's the idea you got?"

"Those general orders," replied young Horner. "The stuff in them about you, I mean. They went out by radio, and unless I don't know my Black Invaders they were picked out of the air.

"They weren't important from a military standpoint so I doubt if they were sent out in code. Now if the Blacks did pick

"THAT'S TRAVIS — — — NICK TRAVIS!" HE SHOUTED.

them out of the air, learned that you had been arrested, and were being held for a general court martial, why—"

A loud shout from the man at the table panel cut off the rest.

"Lieutenant—here! Number Four cell is recording! Look—it's recording perfect!"

Dusty and Jack Horner spun as one man and leaped over to the rear wall. The frosted glass plate set against the wall was no longer frosted looking. Instead it was a framed moving picture of a narrow strip of field in front of some heavy woods, half bathed in the shadows of evening.

Figures in the uniform of Black Invaders were running toward a crumpled shape directly in the center of the picture. The Blacks carried rifles and one or two of them fired at the huddled shape on the ground. Dusty could see little puffs of dirt spring up where the bullets smacked into the ground.

A moment later the shape on the ground was hidden from view as the soldiers gathered around. Presently they parted and revealed one of them holding up the figure of a man. His head was sunk down on his chest, and blood gushed from a gaping wound in his left temple.

At that moment, Carter leaped from his chair with a wild shout of savage rage.

"Damn them!" he shouted. "That's Travis—Nick Travis! They got him—those rotten devils got him!"

Agent 10 grabbed him and shook him into teeth-chattering silence.

"Carter! Get hold of yourself, man! Hear me—get hold of yourself! You can't do anything about it now. It's too late!"

The man, who had been seated at the table panel, seemed to fold up inside. His knees sagged, and the eyes he fixed on Agent 10 were glassing with burning misery. Then slowly he straightened up, swallowed, and squared his shoulders.

"Sorry—sorry, lieutenant," he mumbled thickly. "It got me—seeing poor old Nick. Sorry—I—"

Jack Horner pushed him to one side.

"Go get a drink from the bottle in my locker, Carter!" he snapped. "Take a good one, and straighten yourself out. This isn't the time for any of us to cave in."

DUSTY DIDN'T watch the man shuffle away out of sight. He had swung his eyes back to the C-Ray focusing plate, and was watching with agate eyes as the Black soldiers stripped the clothes from the dead Yank agent and searched every pocket and seam. They found nothing, however, save a few personal articles, which they flung carelessly aside.

"Thank God for that much—poor devil!"

Dusty took his eyes from the blood-boiling picture to glance at Jack Horner.

"Meaning what?" he frowned.

"Meaning that they didn't find any of the C-Ray cells on him," was the tight-lipped reply. "He must have done something with the others he had. Maybe they were busted and he was trying to put this last one somewhere where it would do some good.

"Looks to me like he was chased and this fell from his pocket. Either that, or he threw it away before he died. Hell—why does God seem to put the good men in front of bullets?"

Dusty made no comment. There was nothing to say. He knew that although Jack Horner held himself in check outwardly, the picture on the focusing plate was like a knife turning in his heart. Hell's bells, what sane man can look at the mutilated body of a dead comrade and not feel some pang of sorrow and bitter anguish? But true fighting man that he was, Jack Horner was keeping his inner thoughts to himself. The only single sign of how he felt was reflected in the smouldering depths of his eyes riveted to the focusing plate.

And then, without warning, a weird phenomenon took place that rocked Dusty back on his heels in dumbfounded amazement.

"For God's sake, look, Dusty—that figure that just came into the picture! There—on the left!"

Agent 10's words roared from his throat, but in that moment of complete bewilderment, Dusty hardly even heard them. Jaw sagging, eyes popping out of his head, he stared at the figure of a man who had joined the group about the dead American.

The man was a walking image of himself—physique, hair, features, uniform—Dusty Ayres talking with a group of Black Invader soldiers far behind the enemy lines!

## CHAPTER 5
## MIDNIGHT AMBUSH

"**M**Y GOD, it—I'm seeing things!"
From a long way off he heard the sound of his own voice. And for a dizzy moment he almost believed that it

was his double on the focusing plate, and not himself, who was saying the words.

Eventually he got control of his jangled senses, but he still stood staring wide-eyed at a moving picture of himself. And then his double shrugged, gestured with his hands, and walked out of the picture. The Black soldiers left a moment or two later, leaving only the dead Yank agent in the picture.

Slowly Dusty turned his head, looked at Agent 10. His own dumbfounded amazement was reflected on the Intelligence man's face.

"For God's sake, Jack!" he gulped. "What do you make of that?"

Young Horner started to shake his head, suddenly stiffened and grabbed Dusty's arm.

"Hell, are we dumb!" he exclaimed, pointing his other hand at the focusing plate. "That's the answer to your mix-up. Don't you see—your double?"

Even as his pal started to speak, the truth came smacking home to Dusty. He nodded vigorously.

"Right, right!" he shouted. "He fooled Curly—he fooled the destroyer commander—and he fooled that Captain Wicks at the Army-Navy Club. No wonder Wicks looked at me funny as he went out of the room. The bums have got a double of me. Why—"

He finished it with a grating curse. Jack Horner echoed the curse and slowly pounded his two clenched fists together.

"God, that's one I never figured on!" he grated. "A double of you, and using your special authority. My God, he can snarl up heaven knows what!"

Dusty said nothing. Simply nodded absently. Months ago, by special act of the President and the Congressional Committee, he had been made special contact officer to the combined armed forces of the Government. With that appointment went authority to act in any emergency without applying for permission to his superiors.

It was a responsibility that few men had ever been given in time of war. It was an honor far greater than medals and citations and regular promotion. Seldom had he had cause to exercise the invested authority.

And now, the Blacks were beating him to the punch. One of them had been transformed into his exact double. Hell, perhaps for months that man had been following him around, watching and studying his every movement, tone of voice, little individual idiosyncrasies.

Hell, he must have, to have fooled Curly, of all persons. Why, the bum had even gone into the Army-Navy Club in New York, talked with Yank officers and walked out leaving the positive impression that the real Dusty Ayres had been there.

It was unbelievable—but just the same, absolutely true. A double Dusty Ayres—one fighting for the U.S., and one fighting for the Black Invaders!

"Oh my God!" Agent 10 suddenly gasped in his ear. "That makes it worse than ever. Knocks the props right from out of my plan. Hell!"

"What do you mean?" Dusty shot at him.

Agent 10 didn't answer for a moment. He stood scowling hopelessly at the floor. Presently he spoke.

"You've got to go back to the detention cell, Dusty," he said. "We've got to tell Staff that you have a double—and that it was your double that pulled all that stuff yesterday. If we don't, you won't last a day. Our armies will think that you've escaped, and both sides will be gunning for you.

"I had hope that you and I could—oh, well that's no use now. We've got to tell all about this to Staff so that a warning can be sent out that you have a double. Get a new code number for you, so that this damn double can't pull any more trick stuff. I—"

"Wait a minute!" Dusty cut him off. "What had you planned? Tell me that first."

The Intelligence man grimaced.

"Just a hit-or-miss idea," he said sadly. "With the Blacks knowing that you were under arrest, they wouldn't be looking for you over their territory. We didn't get enough of the C-Ray cells through to our agents up there. So I was going to have you take me up and drop me off by chute. You're the one pilot who would be able to get me through."

HE STOPPED long enough to wave a dejected hand toward the C-Ray focusing plate.

"I had planned to stake one last effort to make something worthwhile show up here," he said. "Getting through their lines is impossible now. By air is the only way—Bersimis is so damn far behind the Front. Oh well, let's go back and tell Staff, and—hell, we can still work it! I must be going screwy. Why, once Staff realizes the truth, you'll be released, only nothing will be said about it. You can get me over and drop me, just as I planned."

"Nix! That's out!"

Jack Horner gestured angrily.

"Now, listen, Dusty!" he snapped. "I know what you're going to say—that we go together, as we have before. But nothing doing this time. You'd get nailed the instant you set foot on the ground. Bersimis is Black H.Q. It's their naval base, and their air base.

"Even with my knowledge of the language and my ability to make-up to look and act like one of them, I'll only stand a fifty-fifty chance. But I've got to go just the same. And you're the one pilot in thousands who can get me over that area without them getting suspicious.

"Now, snap out of it. There's a Black amphibian hidden about ten miles from here. We've been keeping it for just such an emergency as this. Young Stafford was our regular pilot—he's a member of the department. But—well, he's gone now."

Dusty simply shook his head as the other paused.

"It's still nix," he said evenly. "Now, wait—stop letting off steam. I've got an idea that puts yours in the shade. Couldn't be better if it was made to order. "To hell with Staff—I'm through trying to explain things to them. The nit-wits probably wouldn't even believe your story about my double. But that's beside the point. Look—that mug is playing me! Right? Okay, so I'm going to play him! Get it?"

"Talk sense!" Agent 10 growled. "What the hell do you mean?"

Dusty sighed impatiently.

"Look," he said. "The Blacks have a Dusty Ayres—know they have one, don't they?"

Young Horner nodded shortly.

"Yeah," he grunted. "So what?"

"This!" Dusty flung at him. "The real Dusty Ayres is going to pinch hit for the fake Dusty Ayres! My God, don't you see what a perfect break it is? Why, I could have walked right through their lines, because they'd think it was the fake Dusty Ayres. The real article is under arrest—at least that's what they think! Now does it click?"

The Intelligence man stared at him, then broke into a soft chuckle.

"My God!" he ejaculated. "Damned if I'm not going to have you permanently attached to the Intelligence Department so that I can have somebody think for me! Hell, it's great! I'm your orderly, or maybe just a plain Black soldier. We can go up there, find out what the hell is up—maul this double of yours, and remove any chance of detection. God—it's the berries!"

"Sure it is!" nodded Dusty grimly. "And that rat, Ekar, is going to get the surprise of his life and more. Damned if it isn't like a fairy tale. We'll just collect old Curly, and walk away. And will it floor him! Come on! Where'd you say that amphib was? We're traveling, pronto!"

"Follow me!" shouted young Horner, spinning toward the door. Then to Carter, who had been watching them wide-eyed from the corner, "Don't leave here, Carter! Get Hobson down to help you.

"If anything comes through on the C-Ray get in touch with Intelligence H.Q. at once. They'll be able to contact General Horner, wherever he happens to be. And, listen, Carter—the old pep, fellow! We can't let Travis down—he'd hate us for it!"

"Right, lieutenant!" Carter nodded grimly. "I'm okay, now!" AGENT 10 flashed him an encouraging grin, reached for the door knob, but the door swung open in his face and one of the guards outside rushed in.

"Lieutenant!" he gasped. "Hell's popping. We've been spotted. Caldwell and Spears were picked off by rifle fire a couple of minutes ago. I've herded the others into the garage upstairs. It means a slug in the skull to stick your face out the door. What are your orders?"

Agent 10 swore softly, frowned at the man.

"So they've spotted this place, eh?" he grated savagely, as though talking to himself. "And just when we thought we had them fooled at last. Hell—how many of them, Barker?"

The other shrugged.

"Don't know," he said. "The damn darkness—can't see a blessed thing. Shall we radio for an infantry patrol to close in and ambush them? There can't be many."

Dusty touched Jack Horner's arm.

"Who's them?" he grunted. "You mean Blacks—Black agents, down here?"

The other nodded.

"Must be," he said. "We've been getting each other's smoke for days. Wanted to set up this place as one of our main Intelligence communication depots. Somehow they got wind of it, I guess.

"Anyway, we know that some of us have been watched. Nothing definite for us to act upon. Yank soldiers passing us on the street—maybe just the uniform was Yank. Not to take chances, we decided on this place, and split up. And—they found out. Damn, I don't want to call in our troops. That would be like putting news of this place in the papers. We'll just have to wait. Just so long as we don't let them get in, it will be okay. They'll drift by morning, and we can make arrangements to take care of them if they try to show up tomorrow night. You see—that's what they want, or I miss my guess."

Young Horner pointed at the C-Ray focusing plate. Dusty glared at it. He was beginning to wish that the damn thing had never been invented. Because of its value, hours would pass before he and Jack Horner could get started.

And then a sudden thought came to him.

"Are there enough men to hold this place without us?" he asked.

"Why yes," nodded Agent 10. "Even without Caldwell and Spears, there are eight, with plenty of guns and ammo. Oh, I get you—we try to slip out while they cover us? I—"

"I wouldn't advise that, sir!" put in Agent Barker. "They've got every exit covered. That's how they got Caldwell and—"

"We're going through just the same!" snapped Dusty, grabbing young Horner's arm. "Come on, Jack!"

The other held back, frowning.

"Wait, kid! There's no use in asking for—"

"Shut up, and come on!" Dusty cut him off, dragging him through the door, and over to the stairs. "I've done enough talking for one day and night! We're going through, and to hell with them. Your men can handle this place. Snap it up!"

Agent 10 started to protest further, but Dusty paid no attention. He simply dragged his pal up the stairs and into the garage part of the building. The car which they had driven up in, was on the floor and the front doors securely locked. Six men in shabby clothes, and fingering machine guns, eyed them curiously. Without a word, Dusty yanked open the door of the car and virtually threw Jack Horner inside. Then he raced around the front end and climbed in behind the wheel.

"You!" he snapped at the nearest man. "Unbolt those doors and shove them open just an inch or two. The rest of you get set with your guns. Let them blaze away as soon as I hit those doors. Jack! Get down low—keep your head down!"

"Listen, Dusty!" young Horner breathed fiercely. "This is madness! We won't stand a—"

"Sure it's madness!" the pilot snarled at him. "And, by God, I'm plenty mad! Shut up, and keep down. Hurry up, you! Unbolt those doors!"

The last was for one of the agents who was sidling reluctantly toward the front doors. He jumped the rest of the way as Dusty's voice cracked at him. Switching his machine gun to the other hand, he worked back the heavy bolts, and pushed the doors outward so that an inch or two of blackness showed between them.

Instantly from somewhere out in the darkness, a rifle cracked and there was a thud as the bullet smacked into the heavy door.

Dusty thumped down on the electric starter.

"Douse the lights, and stand back!" he thundered.

A SPLIT second later, as the car's engine roared into savage life, the lights went out and the whole place was plunged into pitch darkness. And in that moment Dusty meshed gears and fed maximum hop to the engine.

Rubber screamed sound as the wheels spun, then they gripped and the car shot forward. Its front bumped, smashed ahead into the slightly parted doors with terrific impact, and they went flying outward on their hinges. Before they could slam back again the car was through and tearing along the driveway toward the house.

Behind, half a dozen machine guns clattered out sound. Off to Dusty's left a spear of flame cut the darkness, and something twanged against the engine hood and went whining away. Another tongue of flame, and the side window tinkled into oblivion. A third tongue of flame and the windowshield became a maze of tiny cracks.

Shooting out his right hand, Dusty slammed down the lever that swung it to the horizontal, and in a continuation of the movement snapped on the headlights. A corner of the house swept toward him. He pulled down hard on the wheel, missed it by inches and swung back onto the main driveway. Guns were still yammering behind, and every few seconds singing steel slapped into the car and went twanging off.

At the end of the driveway were two big brick gate posts.

Dusty shot the car through them, left his right rear bumper hooked about one of the posts, and swerved onto the main road. Straightening out, he gave the engine all it could take, and burned up the road in a terrific burst of speed.

"Hey! We should have gone the other way. The ship is at the old New Canaan field!"

Agent 10's wild shout was little more than a faint murmur above the roar of the engine.

"Keep your shirt on!" Dusty bellowed back. "Lived in these parts for three years. I know all the short cuts. Hang on—turn ahead!"

Hardly had Dusty shouted out the last when he swung down with all his might on the wheel and jumped on the brake. The car seemed to let out a howl of protest, skidded crazily around, teetered for a hellish split second, and then shot down a narrow side-road like a high-speed streamlined limited.

Teeth clenched, body bent rigidly over the steering wheel, Dusty held the car on the road, took upgrades and downgrades, and went whirling around winding turns at break-neck speed.

Several times Agent 10 yelled something at him, once even punched him on the shoulder, but he didn't pay any attention. Every bit of his attention was concentrated on the strip of headlight-flooded road continually racing toward him.

Finally, after twisting and turning and doubling back a dozen times, he shot the car clean off the road, through a field, and skidded it to a halt in front of a weather-beaten shed.

"This is it, isn't it?" he grunted at Agent 10.

Young Horner gulped for breath.

"Yeah, yeah!" he managed to get out. "The plane's in there— all set. My God, and you once called me a crazy driver!"

"Save it!" Dusty cut him off as he leaped out. "Think I wanted those bums to tag us? Snap it up!"

"You saw the lights, too, huh?" panted Jack Horner, as they both ran toward the darkened shed. "I yelled at you, but you were too busy with the wheel. But you shook them off damn soon!"

Dusty, who was shoving back the sliding doors, suddenly stiffened and looked across the field.

"We're both wrong!" he shouted, slamming the door back with all his might.

"Snap it up—into the ship—they've picked up our smoke again!"

And it was true. Twin headlights, bouncing crazily in the darkness, swung in from the main road and were now sweeping across the field toward them.

And just above the level of the lights, jetting tongues of flame were cutting the darkness, and yammering sound was punctuating the roar of the onrushing car's engine!

# CHAPTER 6
## DEATH OVER WATER

D USTY AND Jack Horner reached the cabin door of the amphibian together. Jerking it open, Dusty shoved his pal inside and leaped in himself. It was very dark, but he didn't bother to snap on the cabin light. He simply thumped down on the electric starter and breathed a fervent prayer. The prayer was answered in about five seconds. The engine coughed and sputtered, then roared into life.

No time to wait for the back-to-back engines mounted on the center section of the single wing to warm up. The car was less than a hundred yards away, and hot steel, from whomever was holding the machine gun, was smacking against the nose of the hull.

Releasing the wheel brakes, Dusty taxied out through the open doors, swung the craft away from the approaching car, and rammed the throttle all the way forward. Both engines took it without a skip, and amid a hail of twanging death the plane gathered speed and went arcing up into the night-darkened sky.

"Boy!" whistled Dusty, relaxing back in the seat. "These close shaves are getting to be too much of a habit. Some day the razor's going to slip."

"You're telling me?" echoed Jack Horner, brushing a hand across his forehead. "Just about one month more of this cockeyed war and they'll have to put me in a padded cell, sure as you're a foot high."

For a few moments both lapsed into silence. Dusty leaned forward, snapped on the cowl light and studied the instruments. Then he moved the stick over and swung the ship around toward the shore line. Jack Horner didn't realize it for a few moments, but when he did he let out a yelp.

"Hey! We're not headed for England this time, Dusty. Bersimis is due north!"

Dusty made clucking sound with his tongue.

"Why so it is!" he gasped sarcastically. "And here I was thinking it was out in the middle of the Atlantic! Get wise to yourself, kid, we happen to be flying a Black Invader ship."

Jack Horner snorted.

"Sure we are! So what?"

"Oh, nothing much," Dusty grunted. "But somehow I get annoyed when my own side takes a pop at me. And in case you don't know it, our bat patrols have been doubled during the last week, all along the Front. Of course, we probably wouldn't sight a single one, but why take chances when there is all of the broad Atlantic for us to fly over? Matter of fact, it might look better to land at Bersimis coming in from the sea."

"Right as usual," nodded Agent 10. "Pick up the marbles. Only I'd suggest that we didn't land right at Bersimis. After all, it would be embarrassing to, say, bump right into Fire-Eyes taking a stroll with this double of yours. Frankly, I'm getting to like your idea not so much."

Dusty reached for the throttle.

"Want to get off?" he asked. "We're not over the water yet."

Agent 10 cursed.

"Some day I'm going to forget you're just about the best friend I ever had!" he growled, "and poke you one in that mug of yours. Cut the dizzy stuff. Let her rip! As Curly would say—papa's going where mama's going!"

The very mention of Curly's name, brought a flood of annoying thoughts back to Dusty. He fell silent, stared gloomily ahead, and sat so perfectly still that Agent 10 peered at him several times to make sure that he wasn't asleep.

And then suddenly he sat up straight in the seat, half turned, and faced young Horner.

"Clever as hell we are!" he grated. "We forgot the most important thing—some Black Invader duds for you to wear. Hell, we'll have to go back."

To his amazement his pal smiled and shook his head.

"Keep right on," he said. "We didn't forget a thing. Everything

I need is stuck in back there. I'm fussy that way. Always keep stuff in various places, just in case I need it. You whip up the horses while I go into my dance."

As he spoke the Intelligence man climbed out of his seat and went to the rear of the cabin. He was back there about ten minutes, during which time Dusty swung the ship out off the coast for several miles and veered toward the north.

"There!" grunted Agent 10 dropping back into the seat. "Feel better now?"

Dusty looked at him and grinned. The transformation was so perfect that it seemed the work of a miracle hand. But for the twinkle in the man's eyes, Jack Horner could just as well have been a born and raised Black Invader.

"Yup!" Dusty nodded. "I feel much better. As Curly and I often agreed, you're a hell of a sight better looking as a Black than with the real face nature forced upon you."

"Hell, at it again, huh?" snarled young Horner. "I always liked you because—"

He cut the rest and pointed down to the left.

"What the devil's that? Looks like a ship exploding! It is, too!"

**BY THEN** Dusty had leaned across him and was staring down toward the dark waters of the Atlantic below. But in one spot it was far from being dark. There was a shimmering crimson glow about a flaming hulk low down by the stern in the water.

One quick glance told Dusty that the hulk was a man-of-war. And what was more, it was an American man-of-war. Which one, he didn't know. He couldn't see the name on the bow, but he could see the Stars and Stripes at the aft of the boat.

And then suddenly the port side of the flame-spewing craft belched out a great swirling cloud of black smoke and a thunderous roar hammered all the way up to them.

Hardly realizing what he was doing, Dusty shoved the stick forward and went thundering down toward the seething mass. The boat had heeled far over on its port side, and when Dusty was still a couple of thousand feet above it, it reared up high by the bow and went sliding down into oblivion in a gigantic volcano of belching steam and smoke, and long tongues of licking flame. Like a blanket the water engulfed the flame, and in almost no time everything was bathed in pitch darkness again.

Instinctively, Dusty leveled off and started flying around in wide circles staring downward, but unable to see anything but inky darkness.

"What the devil do you suppose it was?" Agent 10's husky voice came to him. "It couldn't have been a mine—there was that last explosion. Maybe a powder magazine, eh?"

Dusty shook his head without turning.

"No," he said. "That explosion looked to me like it happened below the water line. My guess is that a sub did it—torpedoed it twice."

"Couldn't have been a sub!" Agent 10 argued. "Their propeller detectors would have picked it up."

"Maybe," grunted Dusty. "But it was supposed to be subs that got the Fourth Flotilla yesterday. Got every—"

He stopped suddenly, straightened up, and grabbed young Horner by the arm.

"Listen!" he said sharply. "I just had a thought. See if you can figure this out: six American destroyers are sunk without a trace by enemy submarines they know are off shore, and in broad daylight, the Newport News Naval Base is destroyed by enemy air bombs from planes that were not even sighted. And now this battle cruiser just blows itself up and goes down—without even using its radio! Just answer me those, if you can!"

"How do you know the radio wasn't used?" young Horner asked.

Dusty pointed at the signal light on the radio panel on the instrument board.

"There's your answer," he said. "We're so close to that ship that no matter what wave-length they used we would have picked up their signals. And that light hasn't blinked once. Not—well I'll be damned!"

At that exact instant the red light started blinking rapidly. Dusty snapped on reception contact, and began twisting the wave-length dial. A quarter of a turn and the speaker unit gave forth sound. Dusty recognized it instantly—it was the high-speed dot-dash code of the Black Invaders. Though he didn't start to say anything Agent 10 signaled with his hand for him to stay silent.

A minute or two and the signaling stopped. Young Horner leaned back in the seat and swore under his breath.

"Get anything?" Dusty asked eagerly.

"Only one sentence!" grated the other. "They've made some

changes in their code. All I got was—'Will make port by six dawn!'"

Dusty repeated the words aloud, gasped as he suddenly snapped on the cowl light and looked at the station direction finder dial. The needle indicated that the station broadcasting was within ten miles of their present position. He touched Agent 10 and pointed at the dial.

"It must have been a sub!" he got out hoarsely, snapping off the light. "That message was sent from some place within ten miles of our position. I'm betting that it was the sub saying that it would make its home port by six dawn."

Young Horner seemed unimpressed.

"What home port can a Black sub make from here by six dawn?" he asked.

Dusty gulped, scowled thoughtfully out at the dark sky.

"That's right!" he murmured. "It would certainly take some fast traveling for the best sub made. Nuts, this whole thing is getting more screwy every minute. I—"

The rest was never completed. At that very instant Agent 10 let out a wild yell and pointed forward. Dusty had only time to jerk his eyes up, and then slam the stick up against the instrument board with every ounce of his strength.

Something was slamming straight at them out of the black skies directly in front. Nothing more than a big shadow—a shadow that was even darker than the darkness of night. There was no time to turn to the left or right, or to try to zoom up. A plunge straight down was the only hope.

And as the craft tipped up on its nose and started to drop,

Dusty closed his eyes and held his breath. One, two, three seconds of awful hell dragged by. But there was no ear-splitting crash; not even a bump of the wings brushing lightly against anything.

What the thing was that had rushed at them, and why in the name of God they hadn't crashed into it, Dusty didn't know, nor did he try to figure it out at that moment.

When he finally opened his eyes and found the plane still racing down through black sky, he was too thankful for a miraculous escape to think much about anything. Agent 10, breathing raspingly through clenched teeth, was gripping both sides of his seat, as though he never intended to let go.

But the nerve-jangling reaction was only momentary, and in a matter of seconds they were both breathing normally again, though still just a wee bit shaken.

"My God, I'll go nuts if I don't watch out!" grunted Dusty, twisting about in the seat and peering up into the black heavens. "I've seen planes at night, plenty of times—big bombers—but that was bigger than anything I ever saw. Didn't see much, but for a second I thought a battleship was headed our way. My God, but it was big!"

Agent 10 didn't make any comment. He was still just a little too on edge to talk. He simply nodded and sat perfectly still.

Snapping the light on for a second to check his position, Dusty eased up out of the dive and went tearing north at full throttle.

**FOR SOME** weird, eerie reason he had a sudden desire to get away from that particular area. Something mysterious and unreal was up there in the heavens. Part of him laughed the other half to scorn for lighting out in such a hurry.

Hell, he'd scrapped planes at night before—plenty of them. And now, just because he'd almost been rammed by a plane running without lights, as he was, he was getting the wind-up sky high. Maybe it was only a Yank coastal ship, maybe a Yank bomber doing night maneuvers off shore.

"Maybe!"

"Huh? What?" Agent 10 mumbled.

"Huh?" Dusty came right back at him blankly.

"You said maybe!"

"Oh, did I?" murmured Dusty. "Oh yeah, just wondering to myself if that thing could have been a Yank bomber. Damn— I'd like to get another close look at it."

And then, as though the gods of war themselves had heard the request and decided to grant it, a great bulking blur loomed up in the night sky off to the right. At the same instant the red signal light on the radio panel started blinking.

Dusty didn't even see the light blinking. Half twisted in the seat, he was straining his eyes out into the darkness. But a great, indeterminate blur, moving with his plane, was all that he could see.

The very mysterious eeriness of the nocturnal phantom held him as tightly as though by the steel jaws of a vise. His eyes ached from striving to pierce the gloom that separated him from the thing. He even banked slightly toward it, but, as though the other craft were attached to his ship by some invisible rod, it banked away too.

And then Dusty became conscious that Agent 10 was banging him with his fist, and shouting in his ear.

"Dusty. Snap out of it! That's a Black ship. They're trying to get us by radio. Listen—hear that call signal? They're trying to contact us!"

The cabin speaker unit was emitting the sharp, staccato Black Invader jargon. Though Dusty didn't know the language, he could tell from the repetition of various sounds that the same thing was being said over and over again. He sensed, rather than saw, Agent 10 staring at him questioningly in the darkness.

"Has he asked anything yet," breathed Dusty.

"No," was the answer. "Simply repeating two words that mean us—Calling amphibian! Calling amphibian! That's all. If we don't answer he may—"

The Intelligence man didn't finish, and Dusty didn't wait for him to. The savage snarl of aerial machine-gun fire crackled above the throbbing beat of their engines, and streams of jetting flame leaped across the darkness at them from the left.

The pilot of the blurred phantom craft of the night skies had obviously decided to wait no longer, and now he was trying to shoot them down!

## CHAPTER 7
## SILENT DIESELS

E VEN AS Dusty slammed the stick over and thumped down the left rudder pedal, steel trip-hammers beat a savage tattoo against the side of the cabin. A split second later he had shaken them off and was plunging down in a wild spin. A thousand feet below, he pulled out and went slicing up in a curving zoom.

"Hang on, Jack!" he bellowed at his pal. "This crate's too slow to try and slip away from him. We've got to scrap the damn thing, whatever it is!"

Hunching forward over the stick, Dusty strained his eyes upward for a glimpse of the blurred shadow. He spotted it up to his left. The thing was sweeping down at him at a terrific rate of speed. Face grim, body tensed, he nosed his ship around and jabbed both trigger trips forward. The guns mounted on the snout of the hull spat livid flame, and he knew that hot steel was streaking upward, smacking into the weird shadow plunging down.

But in the next moment his heart seemed to stand still. It was as though he were shooting mothballs at the thing. It neither swerved to the left nor to the right. In fact, it made no move to get clear of his savage burst of fire—just kept right on coming down.

Cursing and shouting at the top of his voice, Dusty held his plane in its upward zoom. No damn Black this side of hell, could force him to "back-water" in a sky scrape, and this damn thing wasn't going to be the first to make him.

And it didn't.

With just a few feet to spare, the down-rushing shadow suddenly flattened out and went curving away in the darkness. But in the few seconds allowed, Dusty saw its strange outline.

The body was long and sort of oval-shaped, and the wings

FIGHTING HIS CONTROLS, HE LEVELED OFF · · ·

were curved at the leading edge—curved almost like the wings of a bird.

And although he could not tell for sure in the fleeting space of time, he thought he saw some kind of a streamlined projection on the top of the body, the pilot's cockpit perhaps. If so, it was a damn queer place for a cockpit—right smack in the middle of the thing, halfway between the front and rear end.

Other details he missed. There wasn't any time to see anything else. Fighting his controls, he leveled off his own ship and went plunging forward. But he might just as well have tried to find a drop of ink in a coal mine at midnight. The other craft faded away into the darkness, God alone knew where. For a good ten or fifteen minutes Dusty plowed around in the dark skies, hoping against hope that he might spot the thing again.

That he ran the risk of crashing into it never occurred to him. He was too obsessed with a savage desire to see the thing again to even think of that. He had smashed a hundred steel slugs, at least, straight into it, and yet its pilot had made no effort to fly out of his line of fire.

True, perhaps, the thing was armor-plated, like most ships. But armor plating or no armor plating, only a damn fool pilot lets a hundred rounds bang into his craft without making any effort to get out of the way. Hell, the engines might be smacked for one thing.

Dusty jerked up straight as the thought came to him. Engines! He didn't recall seeing a single engine on the thing. By God, no, he hadn't. Both ends of the oval shape had tapered off to points, and he was sure that there had been no engines mounted on the top of the body. But there must have been engines—must have been.

With a savage shake of his head to brush the tantalizing thoughts away, he snapped on the cowl light and checked his magnetic and permanent compasses for position. What he found brought a grunt to his lips.

It hardly seemed more than half an hour ago that he and Jack had taken off from the New Canaan field, yet they had been in the air for over four hours, and, if his calculations were right, they were just east of Halifax.

As though to check the truth of the dash clock, he turned impulsively in the seat and glanced toward the east. The clock must be correct, for low down on the horizon was the first thin thread of light signaling the beginning of a new day.

Snapping off the cowl light, he swung around and headed straight for the mouth of the St. Lawrence.

"Hey, Jack!" he grunted. "You asleep?"

"No," came the muffled reply. "I've been thinking."

"Yeah? About what?"

"That thing we just had a brush with," grunted the Intelligence man. "I wish the hell we hadn't met it. Something's wrong— something's damn wrong, if you ask me."

Dusty shifted his position in the seat, absently realizing that he felt very stiff and cramped. There wasn't much leg room.

"I am asking you," Dusty queried, "why you wish we hadn't met it?"

"Don't know, exactly," replied the other. "No reflections on you, Dusty, but that craft had it all over this ship. Why didn't he go through with the job and smack us down?"

Dusty shrugged.

"Search me! Why?"

"No can answer," grunted the other. "Unless he wanted us to live for a definite reason. Oh, I don't know—maybe I'm just going nuts!"

Dusty gave him a reassuring slap on the knee.

"Forget it," he said. "I know just how you feel. It was queer as hell, wasn't it? A queer-looking plane, and a pilot who did damn queer things. Maybe we scared him and he decided to get the hell out."

"I hope you're right!" muttered young Horner. And he lapsed into brooding silence.

Dusty made no effort to engage him in conversation. He was too busy keeping the plane on its course and mulling over his own thoughts.

For almost an hour neither of them spoke a word. Bit by bit, the thread of light on the eastern horizon widened, until finally Dusty was just barely able to make out the ground far below.

Ten minutes more flying and they were over the St. Lawrence.

And it was then that fate had its final laugh.

One minute they were running as smoothly as could be, and the next, both engines coughed and sputtered and died out without another whimper!

AUTOMATICALLY SHOVING the plane into a shallow glide, Dusty peered at the instrument gauge and frowned. They still had enough fuel to last another six hours of flying.

Cursing softly, he fiddled with the throttle, fuel-jet control and ignition regulator. But nothing did any good. The engine had, to all appearances, passed out of the picture for good and all.

"No soap?" came Agent 10's question.

Dusty didn't look at him. He was busy staring at the wide stretch of water below.

"No soap!" he echoed. "Maybe the jet has clogged. I'll have to land to fix it. Well, wish us luck. Here we go down."

Steepening the glide, Dusty shot the plane down toward the water below. The river at that point was several miles across. And as far as he could tell, by straining his eyes at the drifting dawn mist that hugged the water, there was not a single boat to be seen. Nor were there any patrol planes in the sky, though he didn't expect to see any. They were still many miles of Bersimis, and there was no reason why Black patrols should fly that far north. However, to be on the safe side, he took a good look as they went sliding down.

Eventually, he flattened out, skimmed along just over the top of the water, and then settled with a swishing thud.

"Lie back and take a nap, kid," he grinned at Jack Horner. "I'm going up through the ceiling trap and have a look at those damn engines. Hope to God I'm right about that feed jet. If not, we're due for a swim. By the way, nix on the nap. You keep a lookout while I work. This mist's pretty thick, but maybe we were spotted."

Agent 10 nodded but said nothing. There were worried lines in his face, and the smile he gave Dusty as he got up on the seat and pushed up the ceiling trap was far from being natural.

Dusty, however, didn't waste time to try and cheer up his pal. He was just as worried himself. They were a long way from their objective and it was up to him alone to get the damn engines functioning again. If he couldn't—well, it meant one hell of a long swim, and an even longer journey across a barren wilderness that was already touched by the first signs of winter.

Pulling himself up through the trap, he crawled along the top of the cabin, and pulled himself onto his feet by grabbing hold of the rear prop. One glance and he knew that he could do nothing without unfastening the side flap cowling. Gritting his teeth, he went to work pulling out the locking pins. That took him almost five minutes, as excessive vibration of the engines during the short scrap had wedged them tight. He finally yanked them free and raised the inspection flap.

Hanging on with one hand, he reached under the twin engines with the other and tried to get at the main feed-jet adjustment lock-screwed into the block between the two power-plants. His arm however, lacked about four inches in length. He tried several times but only succeeded in smearing the sleeve of his tunic with splash oil.

In order to get at the jet adjustment, it would be necessary to take off the engine cowling entirely. That was at least a half hour's work, providing he had the tools, which he hadn't.

Wiping grease from his hand with his handkerchief, he glared at the balky powerplants, and silently cursed Black Invader aeronautical engineering to Hades and back.

A moment later, however, thoughts of his predicament were swept from his mind. From out of the clinging mist came the throbbing beat of an engine.

Instinctively, he threw back his head and peered hard up at the mist-clogged sky. The sound seemed to come from his left; from up the river. And it was low, very low—almost right down on the water, it seemed.

And then he realized that it was right down on the water. Some type of boat, not an airplane, was speeding in his direction. Dropping down on hands and knees, he crawled back to the trap, and let himself down into the hull cabin. Jack Horner had also heard the engine-throb and was straining his eyes out into the mist.

"We're stuck, kid," Dusty grunted. "Can't get at the damn thing to find out what's wrong!"

The Intelligence man nodded grimly, pulled a service automatic from under his tunic front, and glanced at it to make sure it was ready for use. Unconsciously, Dusty reached for his own gun, stiffened and groaned a curse. His holster was empty. The cardboard officer, Major Saunders, had taken his gun. He hadn't missed it until now.

Agent 10 saw the expression on his face, noticed the empty holster, and jerked his head toward the far side of the cabin.

"There's a small pistol in that side compartment," he grunted. "It may do some good. But maybe you won't have to use it. Listen—they've stopped their engine!"

It was true. The throbbing beat of the engine had died out into silence. Dusty leaped to the side of the cabin, flipped open the compartment lid and fumbled around inside. When his fingers closed over the butt of a small revolver, he felt a hundred per cent better.

Turning back he stood beside Agent 10, listening intently and peering out into the mist.

"They may be coasting in," he grunted out the corner of his mouth. "If the sound of that engine meant anything, they were stepping along pretty fast. Probably don't want to risk ramming into us. But listen, don't shoot unless you have to—we came up here to bluff. And I've got an idea."

Young Horner shifted his position, chewed on his lower lip.

"I'm afraid we'll have to shelve the bluff," he muttered. "We're too far from Bersimis. Ten to one only a few of them know about your double. They wouldn't advertise it, you know."

"Maybe," replied Dusty grimly. "But we've got to chance that. This crate is finished as far as we're concerned. That leaves us only one way to get in close to Bersimis!"

"It's a long swim!"

"Who the hell's talking about swimming? Listen, Jack, there's some kind of a boat out there. Maybe it spotted us, maybe not. Anyway we've got to get it!"

AT THAT moment the boat engine started up again. The noise was very loud; didn't seem more than fifty yards away from them. But it was hard to tell because of the mist. Then it softened slightly in tone, and Dusty knew that the craft was running at half throttle, groping slowly around in the blanketing mist. He grabbed young Horner's arm.

"We can't let them get away!" he said hoarsely. "That boat's our only hope. Listen, any signal flares aboard?"

As he spoke he turned around, searching for a signal flare box. Agent 10 reached out and pulled him back as he started toward the rear of the cabin.

"Don't be a fool!" he snapped. "There may be ten or a dozen men aboard the thing. If they don't know about your double, we won't stand a hope in hell!"

Dusty shook himself free, glared at his pal.

"Don't be dumb, Jack! I tell you, this crate's finished for us! My God, do you want to float around here all day? I don't give a damn how many are aboard the boat. We've got to get to Curly.

"You know their lingo—if you see that the bluff won't work, give me the nod, and I'll act as your prisoner. Anything, just so as we get that thing close. Now, shut up, have we any signal flares?"

At that moment he spotted the flare box under Jack Horner's seat. Stooping down he flipped up the lid, pulled out the signal pistol, and rammed the first flare he touched into the loading chamber.

Jack Horner grunted something as he straightened up and slammed back the glass cowl of the cockpit. Dusty didn't even look at him. He shoved the pistol up through the opening, and pulled the trigger. The pistol gave a loud pop, and a ball of blue fire went arcing up into the mist.

Seconds later a harsh, rasping voice echoed through the mist. Dusty turned to Agent 10.

"They've seen us!" he said hoarsely. "Some sort of a hail wasn't it? Answer them, Jack! For God's sake answer them! We've got to get them alongside!"

The Intelligence man shrugged helplessly, cupped his free hand to his mouth, and bawled out something in Black Invader jargon. Pistol ready, but held down out of sight, Dusty strained his eyes out into the mist. From out of it came the harsh sounds of a man yelling something.

"Let another one go, Dusty!" said Agent 10. "He wants us to shoot another flare!"

Dusty dived his hand into the flare box, grabbed a cartridge and shoved it into the loading chamber of the flare gun. A few seconds later a brilliant red ball of flame arced up from the muzzle of the flare gun. Dropping the flare gun on the seat, Dusty switched the pistol to his right hand and waited.

Five, ten, fifteen seconds dragged by, and then out of the mist came a blurred shadow—a blurred shadow that gave forth a low throbbing note. Little by little it took on the sharp outline of the prow of a motorboat. A dim figure was crouched on the bow. Suddenly he moved, called out something. The throbbing beat died away into silence, and a knife-like prow slid in close to the hull of the amphibian. A few seconds more and the boat was alongside, the figure on the bow fending it clear of the metal hull with a boat hook.

Standing in back of Agent 10, Dusty peered at it with narrowed eyes. He could see the boat clearly now. It was a high-speed coastal patrol boat, with single forward rapid-fire four-pounder gun that could be loaded and fired from the hooded armor-plated cockpit at the stern. He wasn't sure, but he believed that the craft contained only three men—one on the bow and two in the cockpit aft.

Seconds later, he was sure of that, and his heart leaped. Two figures crawled out from the cockpit, and joined the third on the bow. All three of them were jabbering at Agent 10, who was leaning out over the hull cockpit opening.

What they were saying, Dusty didn't know, but he guessed from Agent 10's gestures, as he replied in their own language, that they were asking if they could help.

At any rate, a moment or so later, the Blacks on the patrol

boat pulled their craft in so that its side was rubbing against the hull of the amphibian, and one of them climbed up on the wing.

Without taking his eyes off the two that remained, Dusty listened to the one who had gone up on the wing. He was doing something to the engines, by the sound. But presently, he called out something to those down on the boat. They shrugged and said something to Jack Horner.

And it was at that moment that one of them leaned forward and appeared to see Dusty for the first time. His jaw dropped open, and an utterly blank look came into his cruel-featured face. Then he let out a roar and pointed.

Dusty was on the point of swinging up his pistol, when Agent 10 moved like a streak of lightning. He reached out, and knocked the man's hand down, snarled something at him, and spun on Dusty.

"Bluff, no good!" he hissed softly. "You're my prisoner!"

By now the man on the wing had scrambled down and the three Blacks, hands on their half holstered guns, were glaring in at Dusty with murderous eyes.

"We go the rest of the way by boat, my dog friend! Out— ahead of me, unless you wish to die here!"

Agent 10's gun jabbing into Dusty's ribs, hurt plenty. But it was the man's snarling voice that made Dusty palm his small revolver and move over toward the open side of the hull cockpit.

Face blank, but inwardly tensed for instantaneous action, he swung one leg over the lip of the opening and permitted the

"DUSTY--- LOOK OUT ---BEHIND YOU!"

Blacks on the patrol boat to seize him roughly and drag him up onto the deck.

## CHAPTER 8
## TERROR BREAKS SURFACE

**P**ERHAPS IT was the brutality with which one of the Blacks was trying to pin his arms behind his back, or because another's cruel grip on his shoulder hurt like hell, Dusty didn't stop to figure which. In any event, the instant his feet touched the deck, he became a whirlwind of steel springs flying out in all directions.

There was no time to shift the small pistol in his hand and get his finger curled about the trigger. He simply gripped it tight and brought up his hand in a murderous uppercut that hit the nearest Black flush on the chin.

The man didn't even make a sound. There was just the *smack* of taut knuckles hitting jaw bone, and the Black went flying backward across the narrow deck to smash into the four-pounder gun and collapse.

Instantly, raging voices blasted in his ears. A great weight hanging on his left side yanked him down. He tripped and went sprawling.

A gun smashed out sound and there was a wild cry of pain. A heavy body slammed down on top of him, and steel fingers clawed at his neck. He twisted and squirmed desperately to get his gun hand free, held tight by the threshing body on top of him.

92

With a berserk effort he hurled the weight to one side and rolled over just as a gun crashed close to his head and something sliced through the slack of his tunic. A moment later his aching gun arm was free. In a whirl of light and sound he was conscious that he was pressing the muzzle against yielding flesh. He didn't realize that he had pulled the trigger until the weight that still pinned his left arm to the deck, seemed to jerk and then go still.

The next thing he realized, he was on his feet and stumbling forward to where one of the Blacks was trying to crash a gun barrel down on Jack Horner's head.

The Intelligence man's gun was gone, and he was lashing out with his bare fists. The Black's gun was on the way down when Dusty's pistol spat flame and sound.

An invisible hand seemed to knock the Black's gun hand to one side, and his gun went flying out from bloody fingers.

He howled, half spun and then fell over backwards and slid into the water as Dusty's second shot plowed through his left eye and into his brain.

"Dusty—look out—behind you!"

Forward motion too great, Dusty was unable to stop and turn. The attempt threw him to one side, just as a gun crashed and a bullet whined past his ear. Something charged into him, knocked him flat on the deck.

He had a flash realization that Agent 10 had hit him, and then young Horner's body was flying across the deck. Half stunned, Dusty tried to scramble to his knees and twist around.

His right hand still clutched the pistol, but there was no feeling in the hand.

And then he heard a howl of rage. Through blurred eyes he saw Agent 10 dive head-first into the Black he had originally knocked cold against the deck gun. The Black's gun belched flame and sound. Dusty actually saw the flame streak past Agent 10's neck, and his heart skipped a beat.

But almost in the same fleeting second, Jack Horner's left hand closed over the gun, twisted, and snapped outward. The gun came free, and the Black lost his balance and went spinning to the side.

**WHAT HAPPENED** next was but a blurred, lightning-like movement on the part of Jack Horner. The Intelligence man's right fist smashed into the left side of the Black's neck. The gun in Jack Horner's left hand banged out sound and flame. The bullet slammed into the Black's chest when he was halfway between the deck and the water, and the impact of the steel slug seemed literally to double up the man in mid-air. And then he smacked down into the water.

Slowly Dusty got to his feet, stumbled toward Jack Horner. The Intelligence man was in a sort of daze. He gaped at Dusty, fingered the side of his neck that was completely pitted with burned powder. The sight of Dusty moving toward him seemed to snap him out of his trance. He stiffened, glanced quickly around the deck, relaxed.

"God!" he mumbled at Dusty. "Why the hell didn't you give me time to get on the deck?"

Dusty grinned at his excited friend.

"Guess I should have waited," he said, "But one of the tramps spotted my gun, I had to move fast!"

"I'll say you moved fast!" nodded the other. "You nailed two of them before I got a foot on the deck."

"I'll take lessons in moving fast from you any day," Dusty grinned. "Thanks for shoving me away from that slug!"

"And thanks for shoving that gun away from my head," Agent 10 echoed. "But let's get out of here. Maybe that rough-house was heard. Wonder how you run this damn thing? Come on—no, wait a minute!"

Walking aft a few steps, Agent 10 picked up the dead Black, still on the deck, and as though the body were a log of wood, he tossed it into the water.

"Bet the sharks pass up the three of them," he grunted. "If there are sharks around these parts. I—say, the mist is rising!"

Dusty had already noticed that and was running along the deck to the hooded cockpit. One glance at the instruments and controls instantly confirmed what he had suspected. The boat was Diesel powered.

Even as Agent 10 climbed down in beside him he was booting the starter and shoving down the primer plunger. Split seconds later the engine rumbled into life. Grabbing the clutch lever, he shoved it forward. The shaft gears meshed and the boat moved forward.

Turning in the seat Dusty stared across the water at the amphibian, now almost a hundred yards away. During the flight the two crafts had drifted apart. He grinned, saluted, thumb to his nose.

"Thanks for the buggy ride!" he grunted. "I hope you stay there until you sink!"

With that he swung the wheel over and hoved about until he was heading up river. Though the mist had lifted and was being burned away fast by the rising sun, the shore on either side was still invisible.

"I still think we're both nuts!" growled Agent 10, nursing the side of his neck. "We're getting too much luck, Dusty—too damn much. I shouldn't have let you in on the idea in the first place."

Dusty frowned at him.

"Hey, hold it, kid! That's not like you. Besides, you didn't let me in on anything. If I hadn't come with you, I'd have come alone. I like Curly too damn much. He's the one I've been thinking of right from the start!"

"Yes, I know, I know," murmured young Horner. "But you don't understand. If we could have made it by plane, all well and good. But now—listen, Dusty, swing this thing around. It's no use. We haven't a hope in hell.

"There are a hundred Black navy ships between us and Bersimis. Those Blacks told me. That's how they happened to be near us. They and a lot of other coastal boats are patroling the whole river."

"Patroling it for what?" Dusty asked.

Agent 10 shrugged.

"I don't know," he said. "And I didn't dare ask. They seemed to act as though I should know. Hell, I thought it was curtains when they saw you. They obviously didn't know about your double. And there'll be others like them."

Young Horner finished with a forlorn, hopeless gesture. Dusty reached out his free hand, placed on his knee.

"Let's look at the facts, Jack," he said quietly. "We know that there is something screwy taking place at this Bersimis location. We know that Ekar, Fire-Eyes and Curly are there, or were there last night.

"We know that a bum who is doubling for me is also there. All that, added up, was plenty of reason for us to go places and try to do things. We had a forced landing, and by some clever work on your part, we're here in a Black coastal patrol boat. And—"

"Exactly the point!" the other insisted. "It isn't helping us at all. The river ahead is lousy with ships. They told me. And that uniform you've got on—"

"Is the one thing we can hang either success or failure on!" Dusty snapped. "I grant you the idea may be crazy—it may not work right. But the fact remains that here we are—and so what the hell else can we do but go through with it?

"This tub won't take us back to the States. Hell, Jack, it's exactly the same idea that we pulled over in England. We're doing the exact opposite of what they'd think we'd do."

Young Horner scowled at the clear stretch of river ahead. And Dusty drove home his final point.

"Listen," he said, "what would you think if you saw Ekar walking through Times Square?"

"Huh? Why—why, hell, Ekar wouldn't be walking through Times Square."

"Right!" agreed Dutsy. "And neither would Dusty Ayres go chugging up to Bersimis in a motorboat!"

"But the thing that those Blacks thought I knew, but didn't!" the Intelligence man put out lamely. "It may—"

"Right again!" Dusty shut him off. "It may be the thing we're trying to find out! Could you ask for anything better than a front-row seat in a motorboat? Hell, no! And, incidentally, don't worry so much about this uniform of mine.

"This cockpit hood practically covers us. We'll do the worrying about the uniform when we finally get ashore. Buck up, kid! There are two of us, and the old Yank luck is going to see one of us through—don't ever forget that, either!"

Jack Horner's made-up features twisted into a slow smile. He raised his hands, palms front, in a gesture of complete and final surrender.

"I guess you're right, Dusty," he said. "Yeah, I guess you are. It was just that there seemed to be so many things tripping us up—so much cockeyed mystery, that—oh well, I guess that everything accomplished in time of war is just the result of blind luck, after well-laid plans have gone haywire. Sorry, for the mental relapse. Let me stay in and pitch."

Dusty gave him a playful punch in the ribs.

"That's the old fight!" he beamed. "Knew I just had to get your dander up, that's all!"

Turning front he heaved an inward sigh, and scanned the

surface of the river, The mist had disappeared almost entirely now, and the shore line was but a dull mark on either side.

Straight ahead there was nothing but water—gray-green water that was beginning to glisten and shimmer in the rays of the sun burning down through the last of the mist.

FOR AN hour or more the scene remained just the same, except that on four different occasions when they spotted other coastal patrol boats sliding along closer in toward the shore.

Each time they virtually held their breath, and waited anxiously for any of the craft to veer around and come speeding out to them. But it seemed that the other boats had a definite beat to patrol, or else their crews had not sighted them.

By the time they had passed the fourth group hope was beating high in Dusty. When one partol boat wasn't interested in another patrol boat, why should the bigger ships, farther ahead? Spur-of-the-minute logic, perhaps, but it served to make Dusty feel a darn sight better than he really had when he had argued with Jack Horner.

The Intelligence man's spirits had picked up considerably, too. And although his face was grim, a faint grin tugged at the corners of his mouth.

Yes, hope was running high. Everything was going along without a single hitch. Another hour and they would sight the river city of Bersimis.

Such was Dusty's thought as he leaned forward and peered up through the cockpit hood-slit toward the sky. And it was at that moment that he saw it—a Black Invader navy plane streaking down toward them at full speed.

An instant later he heard the wild, thunderous roar of an over-reving engine. Instinctively he turned and glanced back, but there was nothing to see but water.

An eerie chill gripped him when he glanced back up at the plane again. For some unknown reason its pilot was hurtling down through the air at them, as though their patrol boat was a Yank plane.

"Hold everything, Jack!" Dusty barked. "Here comes company, and damned if I know why. Maybe he's just trying to be funny and give us a straffe!"

Young Horner leaned forward and peered up through the slit on his side of the cockpit.

"Hey—look! He's leaning out, waving—trying to wave us away!"

The Intelligence man's shout was unnecessary. Dusty hadn't taken his eyes off the diving plane. He could see the figure leaning out of the cockpit window, waving his free hand frantically. It was as though the Black were trying to signal something to them. Every few seconds he stopped waving long enough to point downward.

"The guy's nuts!" yelled Dusty, taking his eyes off the plane long enough to look over the surface of the river. "What the hell's he pointing at? There isn't a damn thing here except us!"

Young Horner made no comment. There wasn't anything to say. The Black pilot's wild motions meant nothing to them. A few moments later the plane went careening past, not a hundred feet above them.

Then it banked sharply and came streaking back. The pilot

cut his throttle, and sound slapped down at them. But it was muffled, and as Dusty glanced questioningly at Agent 10, young Horner shook his head and shrugged.

"What in hell can that guy mean?" mumbled Dusty, more to himself. He doesn't suspect us, or he'd open fire. And he doesn't want any help—making no effort to land."

The Black plane was now acting as though its pilot had gone plumb crazy. Back and forth it roared over the patrol boat; each time a few feet lower until finally the pontoon was missing the cockpit by inches. And all the time the pilot was waving his free arm and pointing down toward the water.

Suddenly the boat gave a sudden lurch to the side. There was a rumbling, crushing sound under the keel. Dusty was flung headlong to the floor. He thought he heard Agent 10 yell something, but he wasn't sure.

The boat seemed to have swung into a seething vortex of a maelstrom. Like a chip of wood in a raging sea it was flung this way and that. Through at watery blur, Dusty saw the cockpit flooring split apart, and a fountain of river water spew up through. He dodged it, grabbed for the guard rail, missed and went spinning back over the steersman's seat.

And then as he fought for a hold, the stern rose high in the air, and the boat turned turtle. He sensed, rather than saw Jack Horner's body go flying clear. Directly below him a glistening knife-edged snout was slicing up out of the water, and cutting through the bottom of the boat as though it were so much cheese.

Hanging by one hand to the guard rail of the upside-down

boat, Dusty could do nothing but stare blankly at the glistening phantom rising up out of the water.

The water was boiling with foam, and from the glistening snout spewed blinding acrid smoke. It gushed up into Dusty's face, choked and gagged him. His eyes burned and he was no longer able to see anything.

"So that was—what the guy meant! A sub—a sub was breaking surface—didn't see us—caught us square in the stern with its diving fin!"

Words coming from miles away! Dusty was hardly conscious that his own lips were saying them. Acrid smoke and icy spray engulfed him. He sensed that he was dropping, flung out his free hand for an extra hold—and realized that the turn-turtle patrol boat was falling back into the water.

The icy hardness swept up and crashed against him. Stars, moons, sun and earth whirled around in front of his eyes in one great fantastic display of spinning lights.

He thought he heard Jack Horner's voice—hoarse, choking. He tried to call out, but couldn't. His tongue was stuck to the roof of his mouth. His head was no longer on his shoulders. It was separate, and soaring away through centuries of blasting light.

No! His head was there. It was his body that was gone. He couldn't feel anything. No hands—no legs—no body! Just his head, and a thousand devils from hell were cutting it open with spears of fire. Hacking, slicing, jabbing at it—

## CHAPTER 9
## FACE TO FACE

WHEN DUSTY regained consciousness again his first crazy impression was that he was staring at himself in a mirror—staring at himself, and grinning pleasantly. And then the reflection in the mirror moved! But his brain, foggy as it still was, told him that he hadn't moved. He knew damn well that he hadn't moved, yet his reflection in the mirror had stood up from a chair, and was walking toward him!

And then the most crazy thing of all took place. His reflection spoke to him, said,

"How do you feel?"

Hell, was he going crazy? Was he dead? Was this the sort of thing that happened beyond the vale?

He closed his eyes, tried to think. Opened his eyes again. And when he did, the real truth came crashing home to him. He was sitting in a chair in a small room. His arms were lashed behind him. He was soaking wet from head to foot. Every square inch of his body felt as though it had been hammered to a crushed pulp. It even hurt for him to breathe.

Those items he brushed aside as they flickered across his throbbing brain. It was the reflection in the mirror. There was no mirror. The reflection was a human being—his living double, garbed in natty dry clothes, and a mile-wide grin on his face.

"You—you bum—so it's you!"

Dusty choked out the words as his blood reached the boiling point in his veins. His double laughed, and Dusty thought he'd

103

go plumb out of his head. The laugh was just like his own. And the tone of voice that followed it.

"I'm complimented, Ayres. Guess I didn't do such a tough job at that, huh?"

The man laughed again, and immediately dropped the pose.

"No sense acting as you in front of you, is there?" he chuckled. "But I just want to say that you owe me a vote of thanks. I saved your life, Ayres."

Dusty stared at him unblinking.

"Yeah?" he grunted. "How come? I never met a Black yet who had any desire to save my life?"

The other shrugged, gestured with both hands.

"You never met me before—fortunately," he said. "And I value your life very highly. While you live, I can do great things. But if you should die—then I must begin all over. You see, it has taken every hour of the day and night, for months, to become you, Captain Ayres. And now—well frankly, I should regret to see you die."

"Thanks!" Dusty nodded. "But your boss may feel different about it."

To Dusty's amazement the other stiffened, and true Black Invader rage blazed up in his eyes.

"Ekar had his chance!" he snarled. "He can no longer command me. Me—I am the important one!"

Dusty started inwardly. Things had certainly taken a crazy twist. He had believed that this double and Ekar had worked together to get Curly. But now, apparently, there was friction between them.

The Black was talking again. His sudden rage had faded.

"Yes, I saved your life, Captain Ayres. When I saw you there in the water I was more than surprised. I took you aboard and flew you back here. Tell me, how did you get into that boat?

Dusty didn't hear the question. A sentence was whirling around inside his head—"I took you aboard and flew you back here." Took him aboard what? Flew him in what?

"You look puzzled, Ayres. What's the matter? Are you sick? Do you want a doctor? You didn't appear injured—just knocked out a bit. What's wrong?"

The last made an impression on Dusty. He swallowed and stared hard.

"You flew me here?" he echoed. "In what?"

The other started to speak, but caught himself, and smiled slyly.

"You didn't see it, I take it?" he said. "So it doesn't matter. Let it suffice that you are here, and alive. But answer my question—how did you get in that boat? There are usually three of our men on those coastal boats—and they never go outside the river. If you captured one alone, captain, I extend my sincere compliments. You know, I'd much rather be your double than the real you, Ayres. You take far too many chances to suit my nature."

Dusty laughed. Half because of the man's seemingly friendly frankness, and half for relief. So they hadn't got Jack Horner. Or—the laugh died in him. Was Jack dead? Had he been killed in the crash? He tried desperately to shove the torturing thought aside.

"Oh, I guess I'm just tough," he said dully. "And most of you Blacks can't stand the business end of a gun. The three on that boat weren't any exceptions. Didn't put up any argument. But seeing that you're full of questions, Mr. Double, I'll ask another myself. Where am I—and so what?"

"You are at the place I suspect you were trying to reach, captain," was the reply. "At Bersimis. But I can't understand how you—wait, I think I know. Yes, in one of our amphibians! I met you last night!

"It was very dark. I thought it was an American ship. I didn't see it clearly until after I had fired on it. You returned my fire, too. But when I saw that it was a mistake I flew away. So—yes, that is how you came up here. You must have landed, and lured one of our patrol boats over. Clever, captain, very clever of you. But another question, did you think that your uniform would not be noticed?"

Dusty was living again the queer episode of the night before. The Black repeated his question, leaned over and touched Dusty's uniform for emphasis. Dusty grinned.

"Why should it be?" he said. "There was one like it parading around!"

That puzzled the Black. He knitted his brows and stared at Dusty without speaking for a couple of minutes.

"You knew?" he suddenly asked sharply. "You knew about me?"

"Knew about you?" Dusty snapped back. "Hell, of course I did. I saw you—saw you looking at the body of that Yank agent you rats killed. In that field, by the woods. Now play that one on your harmonica!"

The other's eyes got wide and foggy with dumbfounded amazement. He started to speak half a dozen times, but succeeded in saying nothing. Then presently a sly, crafty look leaped into his eyes. He leaned forward.

"Then there are others!" he snapped. "Others who met you? Perhaps they stole the coastal boat. You didn't capture it at all. They took the plane and flew away."

DUSTY THOUGHT of how he had cursed the engines of the amphibian for passing out. Hell, he should have kissed them for making him land so far down the river.

It was a cinch that the Blacks hadn't found it yet. And this double of him was losing some of his easy-going manner. Getting just a bit worried about the possibility of other Yanks being around. He grinned, gestured half-heartedly.

"You sure can guess the right answers!" he said. "Yup, that's just how it worked out. Three or four thousand of them went back in the plane and the other two dozen went back to their job at trying to be Black soldiers. Anything else you want to know?"

The other regarded him threateningly.

"Much as I wish you to live, Ayres," he said coldly, "there is something far more important than my wish."

Dusty took a blind shot in the dark.

"Such as our finding out the little stunt you're pulling here at Bersimis, eh?"

For a moment he thought that the other was going to hit

him with his clenched fist. He gritted his teeth, steeled himself for the blow. But it never came.

Instead, the man relaxed, turned and took two steps toward the door, but stopped dead as it suddenly slammed open and Ekar came dashing into the room. His snake eyes flickered across the double's face, swept across the room and became fixed on Dusty.

The double said something in his native tongue. Ekar snarled back at him, brushed past and came over to Dusty. His face was livid with rage, and his lips were twitching violently. Then with surprising suddenness he relaxed, chuckled softly.

"So you couldn't wait, my dog friend?" he got out in his peculiar rasping voice. "And you came anyway. I warned you that it would be useless. Fool, did you think that we believed that radio communication about your arrest? You have tried your last trick, my—"

He stopped short with an angry curse as Dusty burst out laughing. Then he added his own mirthless chuckle.

"Yes, let us laugh!" he mocked. "It has all been so very funny! And now, it is the end!"

Dusty fixed him with a cold eye.

"Aren't you going to ever get tired of that line?" he rapped out. "O.K., call it the end. But it's also the end for you and all your brood. You're on the run, Ekar—running like hell. And this time you're not going to stop running until every damn one of you drops dead. We know, you rat! Get it—we know!"

The last was a bluff, and Dusty watched his hated enemy's

face as he shouted the words. The result brought some joy to his aching heart.

Ekar, as the other Black had done, stiffened straight and peered at him through narrowed lids.

"You know what?"

The words fairly shot off the man's lips.

"About what you're doing here!" Dusty snapped. "Hell, the Yanks know every move you've made in the last weeks."

Dusty paused just long enough to suck in his breath, and fired his ace card.

"Your whole area is covered by C-Ray cell recorders! Ever hear of the C-Ray?"

For one hellish instant Dusty was afraid that he had spoken out of turn; that he'd given away something that should remain secret. Both Ekar and the other Black looked blankly at him. And then, suddenly, Ekar made soft half hissing, half whistling sound with his lips.

"The C-Ray!" he breathed. "That is what you call it, eh?"

He jammed his hand into his tunic pocket, and pulled out one of the cells. The lens had been either broken by mistake, or on purpose for examination. At any rate, it was hopelessly smashed beyond use.

"That is one of them, eh?" he snapped, holding it out.

Dusty took the bit by the teeth, nodded.

"Part of it," he said. "Not the main part, though. You found it yesterday afternoon when you and your ten-cent boss were trying to pump Lieutenant Brooks, eh?"

If Ekar had been worried before, he now acted as though he

were about to collapse. His copper-tinted hands, gripping the C-Ray cell went yellowish at the knuckles. And the fingers of the other hand flexed spasmodically.

Suddenly he turned and snarled something at Dusty's double. The Black shook his head, snarled back at Ekar. Like two tigers they stood glaring at each other. Then Ekar said something that seemed to take all the starch out of the other one. He nodded, turned on his heel, and went out the door.

Dusty regretted seeing him leave. As long as the double stayed he had the feeling that his own life was in no immediate danger. But now he was alone with a man who wanted nothing better than the chance to kill him.

Yet, as he switched unflinching eyes to Ekar's face, he sensed that the Black was occupied with other things than just the thought of killing him. He kept looking down at the smashed C-Ray cell he still held in his hand. Perhaps a full minute ticked by, and then he spoke.

"So your swine comrades know everything, eh?"

"That's what your boy friend asked," Dusty replied in a hard tone. "And I said, yes. All that is needed is the final signal from me!"

Ekar laughed harshly at that.

"The signal from you, eh?" he sneered. "Then there is no cause for worry. You, my friend, will not give any signal!"

Forcing a grin to his lips, Dusty played the game for all it was worth.

"Think I came up empty-handed, you cluck?" he snapped. "And do you think I came alone?"

He would have gladly bitten off his tongue to be able to take back the last. Ekar's eyes widened.

"The fool!" he hissed. "He should have looked for the other, instead of racing you here to receive his praise from our Great One! Very well, we shall set a little trap for your swine friend, Agent 10. Yes, and we will put live bait in that trap—bait that he would not possibly overlook!"

Dusty made no comment. He suddenly felt as though he had died a little inside. He had only one hope—a hellish, soul torturing hope. A hope that his pal, Jack Horner had died out there in the river.

If he hadn't died; if some heaven-sent miracle had saved his life he would come straight to Bersimis as fast he possible. Come straight to a waiting trap—capture—and death. The gods were pulling all the strings now; grouping the principle actors in the middle of the stage, and smiling their smiles upon Ekar.

"Stand up, and walk in front of me! We will bait our little trap at once!"

Dusty stared at the muzzle of the gun in Ekar's right hand. In that moment the whole world seemed to stop—everything ceased to exist but himself and that rat standing there with the gun. He tensed the muscles of his body, but relaxed almost immediately as a strange inner voice sounded a note of warning—a warning for him not to act the fool—yet.

Slowly he got to his feet, swayed slightly under his own weight, bit down hard on his lower lip in a savage effort to shake off the utter weariness that suddenly clutched him, and staggered over toward the door.

# CHAPTER 10
## STEEL MIRACLES

**W**ITH THE gun inches from him, Ekar followed Dusty's every step, reached around him and jerked open the door, herded him through. It led out into a long corridor swarming with Black soldiers. They parted and stood leering at Dusty as Ekar shoved him past.

At the far end, a guard opened a door, and saluted stiffly. The second door led outside the building onto the edge of a small flying field. There were only three hangars on the field, and perhaps ten or twelve planes.

As Dusty glanced toward them, he suddenly stopped dead, and didn't even feel it as Ekar stumbled into him. At the far end of the line of planes were three of the weirdest craft he had ever seen.

The body of each was of dull emerald-green and shaped exactly like a submarine, except that where the conning tower should be was an oval glass-plated hump. At the forward end, on either side of the nose, were adjustable elevators. There were also adjustable elevators at the rear end.

Between the two rear elevators was a high thin fin and rudder. As a matter of fact, the rear end of the body tapered into the fin and rudder, like the fish-tailed rear end of a high-speed racing automobile. The craft was of the amphibian type, obviously, for it rested on short, stubby retractable landing gear that could be pulled up into the body.

The wings were perhaps the outstanding feature of the craft.

They were of the center-wing monoplane type, one on either side of the submarine-shaped body. But instead of the leading edge being straight, it retreated backward like the wing of a gigantic eagle.

The tip was almost a perfect point, and the trailing edge cut back at an angle to the body, giving the whole wing a sort of V-shaped design.

In the leading edge of each wing, about halfway out from the body to the tip, was a propeller and propeller-mounting housing, but no engine! The driving power for the propellers obviously came from inside the body and was transmitted to the propellers by some kind of a geared shaft arrangement.

In line with the wing, and running straight back along the side, almost to the elevators, was a long, narrow slot. There seemed to be one on the other side, for Dusty was able to see right through the slot to the plane beyond.

A couple of Black greaseballs were doing something inside the slot opening. Suddenly they stepped back, and to Dusty's utter amazement a metal panel slid slowly down and completely covered the opening. Had he not seen it, he would never have known that there was an opening on either side of the craft.

Staring at the queer craft, oblivious to Ekar's snarling voice in his ear, he drifted back in memory to the strange objects he had seen in the sky while en route to New York with Saunders. He also thought of that night fight with that phantom craft out over the Atlantic. Good God, could it be that these—

"Aero-submarines!"

His own shouted exclamation echoed and re-echoed inside

his head. It was true, yes, it must be true. He was noticing things now that he hadn't seen at first. Just under the tail, on either side, just forward of the rudder, were streamlined propeller-shaft ports that extended backward.

By peering closely, he could just barely see the three bladed-screw that had been pulled back flush with the opening. And forward, on the under side between the wings, was a projection that must be a torpedo tube. An aero-submarine—there was no doubt of it unless his eyes were playing him tricks, which he knew damn well they were not.

Suddenly, he was conscious of a sharp pain in the small of his back. Ekar was boring him with the muzzle of his gun.

"March, swine fool!" came the snarling voice. "So you lied to me, eh? The surprise in your face proves that you lied. You did not know of their existence, eh? That is good! We will trap the other one, and our little secret will remain a secret. March!"

EYES STILL fixed on the aero-submarine, Dusty stumbled forward. The answer to the mysterious fate of the Fourth Destroyer flotilla was becoming clear now. The ships had been lured out to where submarines were supposed to be waiting.

But those submarines changed into deadly craft of the air, and hidden by the gas screen, they had released their terrible aerial torpedoes.

Perhaps one of them had even stayed under water, and launched its charges of death from under the surface. The details would probably never be known. They didn't matter much, now. Over there by the hangars was the answer. Yes, the answer to the destruction of the Newport News Naval Base as well.

Of course no bombers had been seen. By the time hell broke loose, the attackers were below the waters of the Chesapeake Bay and sneaking safely out to sea. The coastal planes had simply searched empty air.

How they were constructed, how they operated below water and in the air, was at present a mystery. But that they did operate, and with deadly results, was no mystery. The Fourth flotilla, the Newport News Base, the battle cruiser that had gone down last night, were mute and horrible testimonials of what they could do. And for their hellish work, he had been arrested and tossed into the detention cell. God, it was all like a crazy, unbelievable dream. Something too gigantic, too fantastic to grasp all at once. But it was true—the secret of Bersimis, the secret for which Travis, and young Stafford, and God knew how many others, had died trying to find out, was those combination land, sea and air hell-weapons back there by the hangars.

"To your left—halt by the door!"

Ekar's sharp command jerked Dusty back from the depth's of bitter rage and helplessness. They had reached the far side of the field and were standing in front of a squat stone building containing a heavy metal door, and criss-cross barred windows high up near the roof.

Keeping his gun and eye on Dusty, the Black fished with his free hand in his pocket, pulled out a ring of keys and inserted one in the lock. As he turned it, a look of surprise came over his face. He gave a grunt, shoved the door open and pushed Dusty in ahead of him.

"And now, my—"

The Black cut it off with a snarling jumble of sound. The interior of the room into which they entered was empty save for a Black guard on the floor. Dusty saw at a glance that the man was dead. There was a small blood-rimmed hole in the man's left temple and his face had turned a muddy purple.

Ekar brushed past Dusty to stare down at the dead man. For a moment he let his gun dangle at his side as raging, dumbfounded amazement gripped him. And in that infinitesimal fraction of time, Dusty whirled into action as he had done before.

His hands lashed tightly behind his back, were useless. But he had the use of his legs and feet. In a moment of sane reasoning he would have dismissed any thought of action as downright suicide. But this wasn't a moment for thought. It was just a moment for blind, desperate, unthinking action.

Shifting his weight to his left boot he brought up his right with all the power in his leg. The toes of his field boot caught Ekar's gun wrist. The bones snapped like match wood, and the gun went flying off to smack up against the stone wall and clatter down onto the floor.

The Black howled with pain and tried to turn, but Dusty was still in motion. Bent over double, he charged bull-like the two short steps that were between him and Ekar. With ramrod force the top of his skull slammed into the pit of the Black's stomach. Ekar gurgled, stumbled backwards, and fell down to his knees.

In that instant Dusty left the floor and shot his body forward feet-first, like a ball player hook-sliding into third base. His crooked left leg caught Ekar across the chest, and Dusty yanked his right leg toward the left as the impact and continued momentum carried them both down onto the floor. The jar from hitting the floor helped him work his crooked left leg up under the Black's chin. And in that moment he exerted every ounce of strength in both legs and squeezed them together.

His right wrist broken, his stomach caved in and bone-crushing muscle squeezing his neck to pulp were too much for the Black. He clawed weakly with his good hand, tried to squirm out of the choking scissors clamp on his neck, and got nowhere. And then when Dusty threw his body to the side and twisted he sensed something give in the Black's neck, and the man went limp. A moment later when Dusty wiggled himself free and got unsteadily up on his feet and looked down at the sprawled figure, he realized with an eerie feeling inside of him that of the three men in the room, he was the only one alive.

For a moment or two, he stood swaying back and forth, looking down at Ekar. It didn't seem possible—Ekar was dead! Neck broken—he had killed him with both hands tied behind his back. God—that was a funny one! He hadn't shot the rat down out of the air—hadn't buried hot steel in his rotten heart. No—he'd broken his neck with a leg-scissors and body-twist.

"My regards to the Hawk, rat! My regards to the Hawk when you two meet in hell!"

The weirdness of the moment, as the terrible truth implanted itself upon his mind, had set Dusty's nerves jangling. With a curse, he clamped down on them, forced his body to become rigid, and deliberately gazed about the room. What next? He had the answer to that—get his damn hands free.

He shut the door with his foot, then began a slow tour about the room, searching for some edge of one of the stones in the wall against which he could rub the cords that bound his wrists. But he didn't find a single sharp edge. And then he laughed harshly. Hell, he certainly was walking in circles. There was an iron cot on the other side of the room. The underside flange would be as good as a knife, almost.

GOING OVER to it he got down on his stomach and rolled over and over, until he was under the edge of the bed on his face and able to force his bound hands up against the sharp edge of the right-angle shaped flange.

It was nicked, and the nicks were sharp, but because of his cramped position and water-soaked clothes that confined his shoulders and arms his ears were ringing and his head swimming before he had sawed through the first cord.

But finally it snapped in two, and from then on the rest was easy.

For several minutes after he had freed himself he simply laid there, fighting for breath, and forcing his heart to pump new strength-giving blood through his veins. Eventually, he rolled out from under the bed and got wearily onto his feet.

"Now the gun!" he mumbled aloud. "Reckon I'll need it!"

He crossed over, picked it up, and gave it a quick examination. The barrel and the butt were gouged a bit by the smack against the wall, but apart from that the gun was still in working order.

Palming it in his right hand, he started toward the door, but

"SWELL!" BARKED DUSTY AND JERKED THE TRIGGER.

suddenly stopped as a thin bar of silver on the floor caught his eye.

He knew what it was even as he stooped down to pick it up. It was the silver shoulder bar of a Yank first lieutenant. And as he looked at it, the name of Curly Brooks instantly flashed across his brain.

"Yeah, Curly's right enough!" he murmured. "Prisoner here, of course! Must have got that Black and then cleared out. Hell, I've got to find him. He'll—"

He didn't finish it. Perhaps it was this thing that science calls the sixth sense, or perhaps he actually heard the noise outside. At any rate, he leaped toward the door, jerked it open a hair, and peered through. What he saw almost caused him to drop the gun. Coming toward the stone hut, from across the small drome, were three figures.

The one on the right was a giant Black soldier. The one on the left was his own double. And in between them, stumbling, tripping, dragging his feet forward, was Curly Brooks.

The lean Yank pilot's uniform was in ribbons, and although the trio was a good fifty yards away, Dusty could see the red ribbon of blood that creased the right side of Curly's face.

A dozen times he lost his balance, and went sprawling on his face. And each time the Black guard kicked him up onto his feet and belted him forward with the butt of his gun.

Blind, berserk rage gripped Dusty. He jerked up his gun, took a bead on the Black soldier, and had almost pulled the trigger when sane reasoning made him drop his hand.

Closing the door he moved to the side, and stood half

crouched, eyes blazing, lips pressed together in a thin blue line. For the moment, the human side of him had fled; murder was in his heart, and murder was in his thoughts.

Ten seconds of waiting hell dragged by. And then there was the sound of a key in the lock. The door trembled, shook and swung open. A harsh voice snarled something in the language of the Black Invaders, and the huge form of the burly guard, dragging Brooks by the arm, came inside. Right at his heels was Dusty's double.

But at that moment they stopped short. They had seen the figures on the floor. In one voice they let out a roar, and started to turn.

Dusty, though, moved like a flash of light. He darted sidewise, slammed the door shut with his shoulder and held the gun straight out in front of him.

"Rats! Hold it!"

They did. Like wooden Indians both Blacks stood gaping at him. Curly was too far gone to really realize what was taking place. As the guard relaxed his grip on Curly's arm, the lean pilot slumped down onto the floor.

Dusty's double must have seen the murder thought reflected in Dusty's eyes, for he went white around the gills and his tongue slid nervously back and forth across his lips.

With the guard, though, it was different. He was either a fool or a complete blockhead. He stared for a split second, then started to snarl. His big right paw holding his gun came sweeping up.

"Swell!" barked Dusty, and jerked the trigger.

The Black's gun hand continued to swing up, but he didn't fire the gun. A dazed, puzzled look spread over his face. He seemed to almost shake his head, and in attempting it a drop of blood oozed from a hole just below his heart. Then he rocked back on his heels and dropped like a stiff log. He was dead long before he crashed down onto the floor.

Dusty didn't watch him fall. As a matter of fact the instant he jerked the trigger of his gun, he flashed his eyes to his double. No need of taking a second look at the guard. When cold murder was in his heart he never shot to miss. Had he wanted to, he could have put a second steel slug square into the hole made by the first.

Nope! The guard was all washed up, and now there were other more important things to handle.

"This is going to be quick and easy!" Dusty grated. "I guess you did save my life, so I'll even it up—though you do rate what he got!"

The Black saw Dusty's gun swing for his head, and he let out a roar and tried to duck. He was just about six years too late. The barrel caught him behind the left ear with a sickening thud, and he hit the floor like a heap of coal.

Stepping across his unconscious form, Dusty bent down and cradled Curly's head and shoulders in his arms. The lean pilot was conscious, but there was a dazed, glassy sort of look in his eyes. They gaped up into Dusty's face, then swept over the four still figures on the floor.

For a moment they lingered on the form of Dusty's double, then slowly came back to his face again. Bruised and bleeding lips parted in a grin. A loosely clenched fist came up and tapped against Dusty's chin.

"It must be you, this time!" came the whispered words. "No other guy could make such a wreck out of a place!"

And with that, Curly Brooks fainted.

## CHAPTER 11
## ACES UP

IT SEEMED a lifetime of waiting hell before Dusty succeeded in bringing Curly back to consciousness. Holding his pal in his arms he wiped away as much of the blood as he could, and bound up the ugly gash on Curly's temple with his handkerchief. Then, though it made him wince each time he did it, he forced himself to slap Brooks sharply on both cheeks.

Finally, Curly opened his eyes and raised a protesting hand.

"Hey!" he mumbled thickly. "Cut the target practice! I don't—!"

He stopped short, and anger flamed up in his eyes.

"Go to hell you—"

Dusty brushed aside the fist curving up.

"Hold it, kid! It's me, Dusty—the real Dusty!"

Brooks blinked, then he saw the double crumpled on the floor, and slowly sat up.

"That's right!" he frowned. "I remember now. The lice shoved me in here—and everything blew up!"

Lingering doubt still filmed his eyes as he looked from Dusty to the double, and back again.

"Listen, Curly," Dusty soothed. "It's the real me this time. Sure, the guy you and Biff Bolton gypped out of five bucks on that race I never finished. Remember?"

With a rush, color came back into Brooks' face. He heaved a long sigh, and grinned.

"Now we're getting places!" he grunted. "Yeah—only you would remember that! But what the hell? Listen, Jack Horner said you were probably dead. He said—"

"You've seen Jack?" Dusty asked excitedly.

"Seen him? Sure I've seen him. He got me out of here—shot that guard. He was dressed as a Black—clothes ringing wet too. He told me how you and he had—"

"Wait a minute!" Dusty cut in. "We've got to work fast, but first I want to find out as much as I can. You saw those aero-subs?"

Curly Brooks nodded violently, and winced from the pain the movement caused.

"Damn right! That bum, Ekar, even showed them to me; explained and talked his damn fool head off. He—my God! That's him over there!

Brooks was pointing across the floor. Dusty didn't have to look.

"Yeah!" he grunted. "That was Ekar. He and the Hawk are doing a little hangar flying in hell right now. But listen, start at the beginning and give me your whole story as quickly as you can. Feel up to it?"

Curly grinned.

"HELL, I feel so good I could almost kiss that ugly mug of

yours. God, has it been a nightmare! Well, briefly—I got your fake radio call, and took Pointon along. Poor old Pointon! We found a Yank cabin ship on the field.

"A guy was bent over the engine. Thought it was you. It wasn't. The next thing I knew, Ekar, hiding in the cabin, had shot poor old Pointon. And the rat up on the engine had a gun on me."

"Was it this guy?" Dusty asked. "This double of mine?"

Curly forgot, shook his head, and smothered a groan.

"No," he finally said. "It was just some guy about your build, and wearing a Yank uniform. Well, I couldn't do a thing. If I had tried anything, I would have got what Pointon got. And then where would I be? Anyway, they herded me into the ship and tied me up.

"Ekar flew that crate and the other mug flew the cabin job I'd come up in. We headed up this way, but didn't seem to be going any place. The bum made no effort to land. Just circled around and kept fiddling with the radio."

"I know," Dusty nodded as Curly paused. "Waiting to tune in on my wave-length. By the way, what was that shot before he finished his message? Or was it a shot?"

Curly's eyes glowed.

"It was a shot!" he grunted. "Little me almost pulled a Dusty Ayres. I'd got one hand free and lunged for his holstered gun. We wrestled a bit and he won on points—the point of my jaw.

"The gun got stuck in his holster and all I did was graze the side of his leg and smack a hunk of steel into the radio. And then I went to sleep. I think he hit me with a battleship!"

The lean pilot paused again, and licked at his cut lower lip.

"Yeah?" Dusty encouraged. "And then?"

"And then I woke up in this room," the other replied. "A guard was riding herd on me with a gun a mile long. He gave me something to eat, and I felt better.

"And then Ekar came in. It was sometime in the late afternoon. He strutted his stuff, said how he was going to snare you through me, take us apart and throw the pieces to the fishes, and all that stuff.

"Then he went out again. But he was back in around fifteen minutes, and plenty mad and worried. Didn't say anything, just gave the guard the nod, and the two of them took me across the field and into a building. Presto—and there I was before his nibs. Yup, Fire-Eyes!"

Dusty nodded, and didn't take the time to tell Curly about what Jack Horner had seen.

"Yeah?"

"They both started popping questions at me," Curly continued. "Wanted to know where you were. What our troops were planning. Wanted to know where Jack Horner was. In fact, a lot of dizzy questions that no one man would know.

"Maybe they were trying to trip me up so that I'd let something slip. Don't know. Anyway, I got part of their drift—the part about you.

"Ekar had tried to contact you, and had drawn a blank. That's what had him worried. His little plan, whatever it was, was going up the chimney fast. And then, one of the guards in the place let out a yell and grabbed up something off the floor in the corner.

"Dusty, it was one of the C-Ray cells! Boy! Did finding it send them haywire. It was all I could do to keep from letting out a yell myself. Say, do you suppose that room was recorded on—"

"It was," Dusty nodded. "Jack saw it all. But that can wait. Get on with the story."

"They brought me back here right after that. Of course, they tried to question me about the cell. Fire-Eyes seemed to know what it was for. Frankly, I thought it was curtains for me. But, believe it or not, Ekar went to bat for me! At least he seemed to. He argued in their lingo with Fire-Eyes, when that big stiff started reaching for his gun, and convince him about something."

"Probably that you were the one way the rat could get hold of me," Dusty grunted. "Okay. They brought you back here?"

"Right! And then I made another mistake—took another swing at him. I landed on his jaw and the barrel of his gun landed on my dome.

"When I woke up—so help me, there you were! At least I thought it was you. But I must say this for myself, there was something about you that just didn't click. You didn't seem excited that you'd reached me. And a lot of your answers, when I asked how the hell you had got here, didn't listen so good.

"You simply said that you sneaked up and landed, and clipped the guard—just like that.

"Remember, I was pretty foggy in the head when all this happened. If I hadn't been, I would have smelled a rat long before I did. One question did go the wrong way. You asked me if I knew where our agents were, up here; how many, and what was the sign to use."

Curly grinned down at his scratched hands.

"**THE BUM** slipped a cog that time!" he grunted. "I asked him what the hell he was talking about. He muttered something about me lying low, and that he'd be back soon. And before I knew it he had slipped out the door.

"God, was I burned up then at you! You see, the crack on the dome had sort of put the think box out of gear. I just couldn't figure anything. Anyway, Ekar came back again soon after that—and there were more questions about you.

"Well, you can imagine how screwy that made me just after having thought I'd seen and talked with you.

"For no reason at all I took a blind shot in the dark—said that you were going to head a raid that would wipe out the place and his aero-subs, just like you wiped out his radio gas bombers a couple of months ago. That, however, brought a laugh. It seemed to tickle him so much, that he trussed up my arms and herded me over to the things."

"Wait, take it easy, son," cautioned Dusty, as his pal started to slump forward. "Never mind the rest. Take it easy, while I stand guard on the door. Try and get some strength back. We can't hang around here."

"No, I'm okay!" replied Curly with a vicious effort. "Listen, Dusty, we've got to do something about those damn Troposphere Flying Submarines as Ekar calls them aero-subs. God, if we could only get to them! They're hell chariots, they are.

"Ekar showed me the works. They're fitted with both electric and Diesel motors. Carry three men and a half a dozen Tetalyne-gas torpedoes. And the torpedoes can be radio-controlled in the air!

"He showed them to me. Under water the thing runs on the electric motors, and they can launch the torpedoes like ordinary ones. But on the surface and in the air the Diesels run the water screws and the wing props."

"But the wings!" Dusty frowned. "Hell, how can they make headway under water—"

"That's the point!" replied Brooks, "There are openings on both sides of the body. "The wings can be folded back into them and the side hatch closed to a water-tight fit.

"In the control pit there's clutch gear that engages the main Diesel shaft with the driving shafts leading out to the props. By the same method you can fold the wings or unfold them. It's simple as hell. He even showed me that.

"The rats have worked everything out to perfection. Even the diving fins for crash diving can be used as forward elevators when in the air. And everything is controlled from the control pit in the top center of the thing. Hell, Dusty, we've got to do something.

"You know what Tetalyne-gas torpedoes will do! Ekar claimed that they can control their flight by radio up to a distance of two hundred miles. They've some new alloy about half the weight of aluminum and yet Ekar says the stuff's tough as steel. And just think, kid, those damn things can get at their objective two ways—water and air!"

Dusty nodded. He was thinking of the Fourth Destroyer

flotilla, and of the torturing hell those poor devils must have suffered before they died. Trapped in a gas cloud that mysteriously burst over them, they were helpless prey to what followed—the blasting hell of Tetalyne, the most horrible explosive known to man. Death, invisible, unannounced, streaking down at them from two hundred miles away!

"You hear me, kid? We've got to do something! God knows what they'll do, if we don't. Getting Ekar, as you did, is only a little help. Said he hadn't even flown one yet. We've got to smash them sky high so that nobody can fly them!"

"Like hell!" Dusty snapped. "We've got to destroy two of them, and take the other back for our engineers to go to work on! And one more thing!" he said tensely. "You saw Jack Horner? Where is he? What became of him?"

Curly gestured hopelessly, shook his head.

"I don't know," he said. "Don't know whether they caught him or not. He came here, somehow got the guard to open the door. He plugged the guard, and told me to stick right behind him. He only answered one of my questions—about you.

"Said that you and he had come up by plane, force-landed, and were rammed by one of those F-Ss breaking surface. Said that you were dead, he thought. Cut off the rest of my questions. How he reached me, I don't know.

"Anyway, he wanted me to help him swipe a plane, take him back to our side so that he could warn H.Q. about the F-Ss and get every damn one of our bombers headed up here.

"We didn't even get close to a plane. Ran smack into a flock of Blacks. The next thing I knew, your double was belting hell

130

out of me. And then he and a guard brought me back. Whether Jack—I don't know."

AS CURLY talked, Dusty's brain clicked over at top speed. Gone was all feeling of weariness; gone were all aches and pains that had been consuming his entire body. He thought only of the job to be done—the job to be attempted, rather.

Somewhere was Jack Horner. Maybe he had contacted one of his agents—if there were any left alive. Maybe the Intelligence man, himself, was no longer alive. Let the Blacks once find him out, and Jack Horner would surely die. He'd been a thorn in the side of the Fire-Eyes too long.

Fire-Eyes! He was here at Bersimis! Two months ago he had somehow escaped almost certain death during the destruction of Shoal Harbor. But now—the Black Hawk was dead! Ekar was dead! And if Fire-Eyes were dead too—

Dusty left the thought unfinished. He spun around, stepped over and crouched down by the side of his double.

"Curly!" he snapped back over his shoulder. "You've got to hang on, kid! Got to help me see this thing through!"

"Sure, sure!" came Brooks' panting voice at his side. "Hell, of course I'll hang on. What's the plan?"

Dusty was stripping the dry uniform off his double as he talked.

"That guard, Curly—the one Jack got. Strip him. Get into his uniform. Pull the skull cap down over that handkerchief I tied around your head. Snap it up!"

Curly moved with surprising speed considering the terrific

beating he had taken. Rolling the dead guard over, he went frantically to work.

"Say!" he got out suddenly. "Aren't you going to put on a Black uniform?"

"No!" Dusty rejoined. "I've waited long enough to take this egg's place. Now I'm going to—and how! Besides, my uniform's too wet. Come on, speed, kid, speed!"

Had the changing of clothes been a race, the result would have been a tie. In less than two minutes they were finished with the job.

To be perfectly frank, Curly looked like a somewhat battered Black guard. There were still several traces of blood on his face, and the drooping uniform he wore was far from a tailor-made fit. However, Dusty made no comment. There was nothing to do about it.

Stooping over he picked up a gun off the floor, tossed it to Curly.

"Add this to the one you have there, kid," he grunted. "Here's the plan—not much, but we've got to give it a whirl. You and I are my double and a Black guard. We're going to get to one of those F-Ss.

"Be set for my yell—then run like hell for the first one you can reach. You say they are Diesel-operated, so we shouldn't have any trouble getting them started.

"Anyway, once we're in one it'll be okay. I've a hunch those things can laugh at any rifle and machine-gun slugs. But the point is, get in one and get it off the ground. If the Blacks can fly 'em, so can we. Got it all straight?"

Curly nodded shortly.

"I got it! Let's go! I've got a hazy memory that Ekar said something about a special raid this morning. Maybe not—but we're wasting time here."

He started to move toward the door, but Dusty put out a restraining hand.

"Just a minute, kid. One thing more. Neither of us stops, see? No matter what happens to one, the other keeps on going. Get one of those crates—raise hell with it if you can! But by all means get back to the States with it! Right?"

Curly didn't put out his hand in a heroic flourish, or bubble over with do-or-die phrases. He simply looked Dusty straight in the eye and said,

"Right!"

A second of silence and then Dusty turned toward the door. But at that moment he stopped dead. His double was coming back to consciousness, groaning faintly. Reversing the gun he held, Dusty leaned over and with no trace of emotion in his face, belted the Black on the same spot behind the ear. The groaning ceased immediately.

"Why not a slug, and make it permanent?" growled Curly Brooks.

Dusty shook his head.

"After all, I do owe the mug my life," he said. "Next time— if there is a next time—my conscience will feel better. Anyway, I've got a hunch there won't be any next time. Oh, hell, skip it! Come on!"

And with that Dusty pulled open the door, and stepped through, Curly tagging his heels.

## CHAPTER 12
## HERO'S DOOM

THREE HUNDRED yards to the hangar line with its row of various types of planes and three Troposphere F-Ss! The prop of every ship was ticking over, and Black soldiers and pilots were swarming all around.

Dusty's heart sank as he saw figures in the domed control compartment of each of the three F-Ss. His plan had come to him too late. It wasn't worth the risk now.

He heard Curly's muttered curse at his side.

"Tough, Dusty! Damn them! So what?"

Dusty was asking himself the same question. He answered it aloud—savagely, without thinking.

"We're going over, anyway!" he grated. "There's just a chance that we might be able to rush one of them and crown the mugs inside."

"Oke!" Curly grunted. "It's at least action. And God, how I'm aching to slug somebody!"

Dusty moved forward stealthily.

"Keep your guns out of sight," he said over his shoulder. "And for God's sake don't say anything. I'm supposed to be that other guy, and—nuts, what's the use of words now!"

Shoulder to shoulder, they started up the side of the field toward the hangar line. Each step to Dusty was like a year deducted from his life. Several times he had played the part of a Black, but on those occasions he had worn a Black uniform.

True, he was playing the part of a Black now, but the Yank uniform he wore seemed virtually to burn wherever it touched his body. He had the crazy sensation that every eye on the field was fixed upon him. A Yank, in a Yank uniform, walking right smack into a milling mass of Black Invaders! Cockeyed? Just about a thousand per cent worse than that!

But he did not hesitate for a single instant. The part he had counted on playing from the very beginning, was now waiting to be played. The gods of war, or whatever one called those unseen beings who taunted and gored men into doing insane things on the field of battle, had called for a showdown.

So be it! He was a fool, crazy—throwing his life away, perhaps. Okay! In those blind, reckless moments, no price was too great to pay for success.

Two hundred yards from the planes!

The air suddenly vibrated with the roar of reving engines, and two sleek Black Darts went whipping across the field, and streaked up into blue sky that was gradually being overcast by slate-colored storm clouds. A few seconds later a third plane, this time a cabin job, raced over the field and zoomed up.

Instinctively, Dusty quickened his pace. A fourth plane tore away—a fifth and a sixth. And then three more went off in close V-formation. Only one plane remained, besides the three Troposphere F-Ss. It was a giant, high-speed center-winged bomber. As Dusty looked at it, the idling propellers became spinning discs of whirling light. But the craft did not roll out onto the field. Instead, it swung around to the right and taxied up the tarmac toward a small group of administration buildings at the far end.

And then, as Dusty happened to look at the group of figures standing in front of those buildings, he stopped dead in his tracks. Behind him, Curly stopped just in time.

"What's up, Dusty?"

Dusty didn't bother to turn.

"Over there by those buildings! You see what I see—that devil on the right?"

Curly made a queer snarling noise in his throat and seemed to catch his breath.

"God! By God—it's him—Fire-Eyes!"

And it was. Towering over the group was Fire-Eyes, the murdering high commander of the Black Invader forces; Fire-Eyes, the single pivot point about which revolved an entire world gone mad with terror, slaughter, death.

Even though the distance was considerable, Dusty could see the stiff green mask that covered the mysterious man's face. He couldn't see the blazing orbs of eyes behind the slits, for which the man was named. But he didn't have to; memory of several close-up views of the black-uniformed devil was stamped forever on his brain.

Fire-Eyes!

SIGHT OF the would-be destroyer of the world's civilization blasted all thought of the Troposphere F-Ss from Dusty's head. He forgot everything in fact, save that Black giant far over in the opposite corner of the field.

Without knowing that he was doing it, he pulled his gun from his holster and took three steps forward. Three steps only, because Curly had grabbed hold of him by then.

"Hold it! Don't be a fool! You know bullets can't kill him!"

Curly's snapping voice jerked Dusty back to his senses. Yeah, Curly was right. Bullets could not harm Fire-Eyes. Many had found out to their own sorrow—and immediate death. The Black commander wore a bullet-proof uniform. Rumor said that, at least, and rumor must be truth, for men had shot at Fire-Eyes at blank range, and the Black was still living.

"Thanks, kid," mumbled Dusty thickly. "God, if I only had a machine gun with armor-piercing slugs I'd be glad to cash in, just to riddle that devil!"

"Well, you haven't!" Curly snapped. "And you'd be too late anyway. Look! He's getting into the plane!"

Dusty was already looking—watching the giant figure stride toward the taxiing bomber, and start to climb in through the extra large door as the plane was braked to a halt.

But he was only half into the plane when something happened. Above the throbbing beat of the four engines mounted atop the single high wing came the savage yammer of a machine gun. And to Dusty's amazement Fire-Eyes staggered back onto the ground, slumped down onto one knee, and clutched at his right shoulder with his gauntleted right hand.

One long burst and then the sound of machine-gun fire ceased abruptly. In its place arose the roaring of many voices. Half a dozen figures piled out through the open door and grouped themselves about Fire-Eyes. But only for a moment.

AS THE MACHINE GUN YAMMERED
FIRE-EYES STAGGERED BACK.

With a bellow of rage that carried clear over to where Dusty and Curly stood rooted to the ground, the Black commander leaped up to his feet and swept the others aside as though they were so many paper dolls.

Bending over he leaned in through the wide door, and then dragged out the limp body of a Black soldier. Holding the drooping man out at arm's length, Fire-Eyes thundered sound that seemed to shake the very heavens and earth. And then he hurled the figure down onto the ground, shouted what seemed like an order, and went stalking over to one of the administration buildings and disappeared.

Those left behind, fired several shots at the huddled figure on the ground, then marched off in the wake of their supreme commander.

Not until they disappeared through the door that Fire-Eyes had entered, did Dusty realize that he was holding his breath and that his lungs burned from the effort. Slowly he let the air out, turned and looked into Curly's eyes.

"Curly!" he breathed huskily. "Do you suppose—do you think that it was—"

Somehow he couldn't say the rest. Curly Brooks understood, however. The lean pilot's eyes became gleaming pinpoints of flame, and his bruised and cut lips flattened back against his teeth.

"Jack Horner!" he got out hoarsely. "It must be Jack—he saved my life. Why, damn their rotten hides, I'll—"

Face livid with rage, Curly started forward, tugging at his

gun. In that moment Dusty leaped in front of him and blocked his path.

"Curly!" he snapped. "Don't be a blasted fool!"

The lean pilot was trembling like a leaf. His eyes were blazing like a madman's.

"One side, Dusty!" he yelled. "Don't you understand—that was probably Jack! They killed him—shot him!"

It was the hardest thing that Dusty had ever done in his life. His own heart was a lump of lead in his chest. He, too, was sure that the figure Fire-Eyes hurled to the ground was Jack Horner. But neither he nor Curly could do anything on that side of the field. Their job was one that might mean thousands of lives, not just one life.

He shook Curly hard, held him in a steel grip.

"We've got to, Curly!" he said bitterly, "We've got to carry on with our part. I feel just as bad as you do. But we can't try to help Jack now. It's too late, Curly—too late. We've our own job to do!"

Curly was still trying to pull himself free from Dusty's grasp. But he did not have the strength. And as he relaxed sane reasoning seemed to return.

"All right—all right," he said heavily. "But God—to think—to think that Jack—"

"Shut up, damn you, shut up!" Dusty groaned. "Another moment and we'll both go haywire. Come on—we've got to be moving. Look, most of them are leaving the ships, running down the tarmac. Our one chance is now!"

Dusty cursed and started walking rapidly toward the Troposphere F-Ss. Only a handful of Blacks remained near them now. And even they were all looking toward the administration buildings at the far end of the tarmac.

But Dusty was still a good hundred yards from the hangar line, when suddenly he saw a running figure off to the left. It was a Black soldier, and the man was running toward them. His hand flew to his holstered gun, but he didn't touch it. A shot now would probably mean the end of everything.

Curly Brooks had also seen the running figure and his narrowed questioning eyes whipped around to Dusty's face. Dusty read the question and shook his head.

"Too risky!" he shot out the corner of his mouth. "Got to bluff to the last possible second—in case. Don't know the lingo, but he'll know what a gun means in his ribs. Don't act that you see him. Keep walking, kid, keep walking. We play dumb until he gets in close to us. Watch it!"

The running figure was almost upon them now. Dusty could see him on the corner of his eye. Face expressionless the Yank ace continued walking toward the hangar line, but he kept his right arm close to his side, hand pressing lightly against his holstered gun, and ready to draw it at the bat of an eyelash.

Three, four seconds ticked past and then the running figure skidded to a halt and snapped a salute.

And in the next moment Dusty's heart did a couple of loops and a few half rolls.

"Don't act startled! Take it easy!"

JACK HORNER, the man they thought dead, was speaking! It took every ounce of Dusty's will-power not to whirl around and cry out at his friend. It was the same with Curly Brooks, too. Somehow they managed to stop casually, and somehow Dusty managed to give the Black Invader salute as he turned and looked at Jack Horner. The Intelligence man was wearing a different uniform—a dry one. His thin lips grinned slightly, then he stepped close.

"They're watching us!" he breathed in a low voice. "Act the officer, Dusty! Curly! Two paces to the rear!"

"God, we thought that—"

"Cut it!" Jack Horner shut Dusty off.

Then the Intelligence man half turned and pointed off the field, back in the direction from whence he had come. Dusty looked and saw nothing but the small woods that bordered the field. He frowned at Jack Horner as the man faced him again!

"That was just for their benefit!" young Horner hissed. "Now follow me! No, no—walk along beside me. Curly! Pull up at the rear."

A hundred different questions hovering on the tip of his tongue, Dusty however held them in check, and walked at Jack Horner's side as the man set out at a rapid pace. Not until they were in the woods did the Intelligence man stop and relax.

"God, I was afraid I'd miss you!" he gasped. "I didn't dare run straight across the field after I spotted you from that guard house."

"You've been there?" Dusty asked.

The other nodded at Curly.

"Tried to get back for him," he said. "Didn't know about you. Sorry I couldn't help you when we met those tramps, Curly.

But it was my play to be one of them. Thought it was my only hope. I figured to come back as soon as I could."

He stopped short, looked at Dusty.

"I saw Ekar's body," he said grimly. "Good work. No, never mind the details now. By the way, did you hear the shot?"

"Shot?" Dusty frowned. "What shot?"

"Good!" nodded Jack Horner. "I was afraid I shouldn't have done it. Didn't realize, as a matter of fact."

"What the hell are you talking about?" Curly Brooks put in.

"There's just Dusty left," was the grim reply. "His double's gone. Call it murder—but I'm thinking of those poor devils in the Fourth Flotilla. Maybe I'm wrong, but when I added it up, he seemed to be the answer."

"He was," said Dusty. Then, "But listen, someone shot Fire-Eyes! We thought it was you, and—"

"Yes, I know," the Intelligence man broke in. "One of the bravest men I ever knew did that. One of ours. He was working with Travis. I met him shortly after they got Curly. He had a hunch and was giving the sign. That's how I was able to mingle in and lose myself in the mob that jumped Curly. They had eyes only for Curly, and when Faber, that was his name, got my answering signal, he worked me out to the edge of the gang, and we were able to beat it."

The Intelligence man stopped, clenched his teeth, and for a moment cast narrowed eyes around.

"Faber, God rest him, told me the true story," he said suddenly. "This isn't the concentration point of the Black Invader forces. At least it isn't going to be after today. Fire-Eyes and

Black Staff are leaving—going back to Europe to make arrangements for an intensive air and navy drive against us sometime in the Spring.

"Only the ground troops and part of the air force is going to remain here during the winter. Those F-Ss are under the command of a Black called Zytoff. They are to make raids on our Atlantic fleets during the winter.

"More of them are being manufactured, right here at Bersimis. The factory is on the river front. I don't know who Zytoff is. Faber said that he had not arrived here yet. He was scheduled to take Ekar's place. It seems that rat had lost favor with Fire-Eyes. Well, the hell with him now."

"But are you sure that it was Faber who—"

Agent 10's quick nod of the head stopped Dusty's question.

"Positive, now," said young Horner bitterly. "Here's the point. Faber said he was sure he got one message through to Washington H.Q. early this morning saying that Fire-Eyes was going back to Europe by air, and about these F-Ss.

"He hadn't met me then, and only held out one hope—the hope that our bombers could smash this place and perhaps cut down Fire-Eyes' retreat to Europe. It was a matter of holding Fire-Eyes here as long as he could. He didn't say how he would, just told me that he could. In case he failed, there was one other way—that was to be my job."

The Intelligence man swung his arm around and pointed back through the woods.

"Their Tetalyne and gas stores are back there in buildings under heavy guard," he said. "But if a man could get through—

one small chemical-fire bomb would set off the whole works. It would rock this place to hell and gone—and before the survivors could leave, our bombers might arrive in time to finish the job."

Agent 10 reached into the big pocket of his tunic and pulled out an object that looked like an over-sized fountain pen. At one end was a little screw cap.

"One full twist and it lets go in four seconds!" he muttered. "Faber tried and lost, poor devil. If he'd only told me. I didn't know he was going to do it that way. A portable machine gun, probably hidden under his tunic. Fired too soon, I guess—only got that devil in the shoulder. That won't stop him long—but I will!"

Dusty sucked in his breath, grabbed young Horner by the arm.

"You mean—that you intend to take that—"

"Past the guards at those stores buildings?" Agent 10 finished evenly. "Yes! Faber did his job—and by God I'm going to do mine!"

## CHAPTER 13
## DUSTY TAKES COMMAND

FOR A long moment a tense, electrically charged silence settled over the trio grouped together in the dense under-foliage of the woods. The very branches of the trees seemed to stop swaying in the gentle morning breeze that drifted across the face of the earth.

In the distance, out on the field, there was still the low murmur of props ticking over. But apart from that, there didn't seem to be another sound for miles around.

STILL HOLDING onto Agent 10, Dusty bored him with his eyes as countless thoughts raced around in his head. As though it were but a matter of stepping down to the corner store for a pack of cigarettes, young Horner had calmly inferred that he was going to blow a mass of Blacks sky high, and himself along with them. A cool, unhurried statement that sealed his existence in this world.

Dusty suddenly shook his head.

"No you're not, Jack!" he said flatly. "There are other ways."

"There are no other ways," replied the other doggedly. "The explosion will hold them for a while. They'll be afraid to leave. In the mix-up that follows, I'm counting on you and Curly to get one of the Troposphere F-Ss, and destroy the rest of the field, and the submarine factory. Then you can breeze home. Once you get one of them back home, our engineers can copy them and—"

"Right!" cut in Curly Brooks. "And you're going to help us take it back home. Hell, be sensible, Jack. Supposing you do blow up their stores? You'll only be tossing your life away for a temporary delay. And—"

"He's right!" Dusty carried on the argument. "Look at it this way, Jack. Our bombers might get Fire-Eyes and his brood, if they arrived in time. You might delay things by cashing in your own life. And then again, Curly and I might not get off in time, and we and the F-Ss might go up along with you.

"Don't get me wrong, I'm not thinking of Curly and myself, you know that. The main thing is to wreck as many things as we can around here, and get one of the F-Ss back to our engineers!

"Hell, supposing we destroy the three of them here? They can build others—build them over in Europe. But with our engineers being able to build them too—then that'll make both sides even. See what I mean?"

"Yes," said Agent 10 reluctantly. "But our bombers—"

"May or may not come!" Dusty shut him off. "Maybe Faber's message did get through, and maybe it didn't. As things stand now, it's up to the three of us to do the job.

"We've got to get one of those F-Ss; we've got to wreck the other two; we've got to smash up the sub factory—and we've got to stop Fire-Eyes from getting away. But first we've got to get one of those F-Ss!"

Dusty stopped long enough to suck in his breath, then hurried on.

"Hell, Jack, you're the key man in our being able to do it! Maybe Curly and I could swing it alone. But with you along, it'll be a cinch. You know the language! You can bellow for them to step aside. You know—any old kind of an order, just so long as we can get close enough to the crate to rush it. Come on—we're wasting precious seconds right now. Should have carried on, when you joined us out there on the field."

As Dusty spoke the last, he started to pull young Horner forward. At the same time he caught Curly's eye and gave him a quick, meaning nod. The lean pilot dropped quickly into step with them.

"Damn right!" he said grimly. "This is the best way to settle the thing—and settle it quick."

The Intelligence man hung back for only a second.

"You're both liars!" he said. "But maybe there is something to your idea, Dusty. If we can only—"

He didn't finish.

At that moment there came the roar of an airplane engine from the direction of the field. Letting out a yell, Dusty broke into a wild run. The other two pounded after him. Cursing savagely to himself Dusty plowed through heavy underbrush as though it didn't exist.

SMASHING THROUGH the last strip of woods he burst out onto the field and skidded to a halt. The sound of the airplane engine was not coming from the field. It was coming from a sleek Black Dart in the sky.

Engine full-on, the plane was tearing down. Like a streak of black light it came, straightened out and virtually dropped the rest of the way.

Hardly had it stopped rolling than its pilot leaped out, tore across the twenty or thirty yards that separated him from the nearest administration building and dived in through the door.

He didn't seem to be gone for more than a couple of seconds when the door popped open again, and a swarm of Blacks came pouring out. At the head was the giant figure of Fire-Eyes. In long strides he outstripped them, reached the big bomber and plunged inside. The others followed at his heels. That is, all except two, who continued racing down the tarmac toward the F-Ss.

The meaning of the furious action, Dusty did not know. He could only guess. And he shouted that guess as he started pounding dirt toward the hangar line.

"They're going to leave!" he rapped over his shoulder. "Something's happened—they're getting out quick. Don't use your guns unless you have to. Head for the ship on the right!"

Putting on a wild burst of speed the other two caught up with him, and stride for stride they went tearing forward. By now the group of Blacks about the F-Ss were half running toward the pair that raced down the tarmac. Dusty's heart leaped as he saw them abandon the three F-Ss. A perfect break, he thought, if there ever was one.

Digging in his toes he practically flew the last fifty yards and skidded to a halt beside the first ship. In a crazy sort of way he marveled at the size of the thing. It was about three times the size it had seemed to be from the other side of the field—a gigantic bird of steel with a door in its sleek side, just forward of the tail. Snapping out his hand, Dusty twisted the streamlined knob and jerked it open.

And at that moment something hit him in the face. As a matter of fact, hit the whole upper half of his body. There was no time to duck or dodge to one side. It just crashed into him and the impact carried him down on one knee. In practically the same instant a startled voice snarled, and a moment later, he dully realized what it was all about.

There was a Black still in the F-S and the man had been

diving out as he was plunging in. They had met halfway, and now they were a tangle of arms and legs on the ground.

Twisting, he brought up his clenched fist, felt it glance off jaw bone. Then a gun popped out sound, and in the next second he was crawling out from under a limp body. Smoking gun in one hand, Jack Horner was helping him up with the other.

"Quick, Dusty—inside! They're coming back!"

Dusty didn't stop to nod to young Horner that he'd heard his words. He simply grabbed hold of Curly and pushed him in through the open door.

"You next!" he barked at Jack, and shoved the Intelligence man inside before he could say anything.

Then he started to get in himself. But he was just in the act of swinging up his foot, when half a dozen Blacks rushed around the end of the craft, grabbed hold of him and started yelling excitedly.

IN THE split second of time allowed, Dusty realized that they had mistaken him for his double. They were trying to tell him something—pointing frantically at the next F-S. They hadn't even noticed the dead man whose body had rolled under the tail. One Black in particular, a man in an officer's uniform was roaring and trying to pull him away from the door. Through the maze of milling figures about him, Dusty saw Curly and Jack Horner turning in the cabin, and scrambling back to the open door. The Intelligence man was shouting in Black Invader jargon, but he was only succeeding in blending in his voice with the general excited babble.

Perhaps it took two seconds for Dusty to grasp the meaning.

The officer yanking him away from the door was undoubtedly the pilot of that craft and was telling him that the other was his ship. The rest of the Blacks were simply fighting for places in the plane.

It was the most ticklish moment of his life. The gun he held in his hand was useless. There were too many. He was practically hemmed in and Curly and Agent 10 couldn't be of much help. One shot and hell would pop loose.

At a time such as that, one doesn't stop to think and reason. Out of nowhere comes a split-second decision and one acts. So it was with Dusty.

He let out a wild bellow of unintelligible sound, hurled himself loose from the gripping hands, shoved two of the Blacks aside and lunged far enough forward so that he could grab the edge of the open door. With every ounce of his strength he slammed it shut in the faces of Curly and Jack. And at the same instant he roared:

"Lock! Amscray!"

In practically a continuation of the movement he spun around again, plunged through the group of surprised Blacks, shouted unintelligible sound again, and made a vicious "come on" motion with his arm. So quickly did he move that he was racing around the end of the plane before the Blacks realized that he meant for them to follow him.

Heart in his throat—expecting with every second to feel hot steel in his back telling him that his crazy, insane bluff had gone flat, he pounded over to the second F-S.

Its door was open and a black uniformed figure was getting

inside. Muscles bunched, Dusty practically crashed into the craft, flung up both hands and grabbed the loose folds of the tunic right before his eyes. He yanked and twisted in the same motion. A voice roared, and then a Black pilot flopped out of the open doorway, and went skidding down onto the ground.

The body was still in mid-air as Dusty released his hold and dived into the interior of the ship. Through blurred eyes he saw a shadow moving toward him.

Instinct, and instinct alone, caused him to jerk his gun up and pull the trigger. Its crash of sound, and the scream of pain that came from the moving shadow seemed to blend as one.

No sooner had the shot left his gun than Dusty spun and swung the automatic toward the open door behind him. A sea of rage-twisted faces was rushing toward him. He saw flame spurt. Something whined past his cheek, and clanged against steel plating.

And then he was squeezing the trigger of his own gun, and pounding bullets back into the sea of faces. Screams, shouts, curses and the crashing sound of gunfire filled the air.

A white-hot spear sliced through Dusty's left side. Another burned along his shin bone. And a third ripped his left sleeve from the cuff all the way to the elbow.

His exact movements, he didn't even know himself. The whole world had become a whirling conglomeration of spitting flame and roaring, screaming voices. He only realized that he had done it when the door slammed shut in his face, and the fumbling fingers of his left hand were shoving the sealing lock bolt into place. Split seconds later he heard the *plunk-plunk* of bullets smacking against the steel sides of the craft. He laughed harshly.

"Shoot and be damned, you rats!"

The last word practically froze on his lips. He was in a sort of V-shaped compartment; the point of the V extending forward and becoming a small flight of steps leading upward. Beyond the top of the steps he couldn't see. But he could hear a harsh voice calling out in Black Invader jargon, and the *slap-slap-slap* of feet running along metal flooring.

To wait where he was, was to ask for death. He was trapped like a tiger in a corner. But one course lay open to him—that was forward, to meet whatever the new menace was. One thing, at least was in his favor. When he met whoever was still in the craft the surprise would be mutual.

EVEN AS these thoughts came to him he was bounding toward the small flight of metal steps. He reached them in nothing flat, started up when a gun crashed and a bullet nicked the lobe of his right ear.

He had sense enough to let go of the step rails and let his body fall. And it was well that he did, for the hidden gun crashed sound again, and a second bullet bored a hole through the air where his head had been a split second ago.

Bruised, aching all over, his side feeling as though it was on fire, he hugged the corner formed by the floor, the V-wall and the stairs, and strained his ears for sounds above him. None came. There wasn't a single sound of movement.

As a matter of fact, the only sound was that which still came from outside. In the couple of seconds that were his, he cursed himself bitterly for not trying to get into the other ship with Curly and Jack.

True, by taking the attention of the Blacks away from them, they stood a better chance of getting off. He felt no qualms about Curly's ability to fly the crate. Brooks could fly anything with wings on it—and Diesel-powered ships were his meat, regardless of type.

But he should have tried to fight through to Curly and Jack. And now he was like a rat in a trap—a steel trap. Having only seen the craft from the outside, and only then from a distance, he could only guess as to its interior design.

He imagined that the steps led up over the water-tight compartment into which the wings could be folded, and led to the control compartment in the top middle. Under the floor upon which he crouched, were probably the tandem Diesels, and the double shafts for the water screws aft.

Just guesses, maybe right and maybe wrong. Right now it didn't matter a hell of a lot which. Along that passageway that led forward from the top of the steps someone was waiting. Hell, maybe more than one. To get to the control compartment, he'd have to risk the singing death that had clipped along that passageway at him. The roar of voices outside had suddenly increased about four times in tone. He thought he heard the thunder of reving engines, but he couldn't be sure. He only knew that the craft in which he crouched was not moving.

And then, suddenly, a horrible thought struck him. That shouting outside! Did it mean that whoever was in the craft had signaled to them—signaled some other way into the thing, so that he could be rushed and smashed to a lifeless pulp? In his mind he tried to picture the craft from the outside. Was there another entrance?

The domed control room on the top of the craft! Hell yes, there must be a way through it! Of course— When the craft was on the surface of the water, the door through which he had entered would be under water! Therefore, there must be another entrance in the top of the craft!

"Get going, you sap! Get going!"

His words were little more than a grated whisper, but they sounded to him as though he had bellowed them at the top of his voice.

Face grim, eyes agate, he slowly twisted over on his hands and knees and crawled back along the corner of the wall for some four or five feet. Then holding his breath he slowly stood up.

No shot greeted him, even though he was back and out of line of the passageway leading forward from the top of the stairs.

Standing motionless he peered at them in the dim light that filtered through from some hidden source. The flight of steps was about four to four and a half feet high. He could just see the smooth metal flooring that led off—a triangular patch of it.

At that moment bullets smacked against the outside of the door in a steady hammering beat. Perhaps it was just wild fire—or perhaps it was to block any attempt of his to escape by the same way he had entered.

"Here goes anyway!" he grunted savagely.

With that he took two steps and shot his body forward head-first, gun hand flung out. For split seconds he sailed through the air then crashed down on the floor of the passageway leading forward.

Momentum caused him to slide along the steel floor, and he only stopped when he plowed into the limp figure of the Black he had shot. For a moment or two he could hardly grasp the fact that no shower of hot steel was slithering down on him.

The companionway in which he found himself was empty, save for himself and the dead Black. It extended forward for about twenty feet and ended in a second flight of steps.

Scrambling up, he paused long enough to grab the gun still clutched by the dead Black and went snaking forward to the second flight of steps.

He was five feet from them when a black-uniformed figure came tumbling down. A gun in the man's hand was spitting a continuous stream of jetting flame—jetting flame that seemed inches from Dusty's face.

His movements in the next split second were instinctive. He simply dropped like a flash of light, snapped his body to the side as he went down, and jerked the trigger of both guns.

Crashing sound banged and roared along the narrow passageway. His eyes never once leaving the spitting flame ahead, saw it suddenly wink out. There was a gurgling cry, and a heavy body slammed down onto the steel floor. Even as it dropped, Dusty was plunging forward. He leaped over the prostrate figure, and went pounding up the steps both guns pointed above him.

From a dimly lighted passageway he suddenly plunged into a small dome-shaped compartment that for a moment seemed to be composed of nothing but heavy plate glass. It was like bursting out of the dark attic of a house up into a glass-enclosed cupola.

Details, he had no time to spot. Something moved to his left. He got the blurred silhouette of a Black swinging a portable machine gun around toward him. From a long way off he heard his own two guns hammer out sound.

In the next instant the Black collapsed on the floor. The machine gun flew from his fingers, skidded across the steel floor and crashed up against Dusty's shin. He hardly felt the pain. In a lightning-like movement he spun completely around, guns ready. But no second shadow swung toward him. He was alone.

And it was then that he took notice of things.

A SECTION of the dome windows had been folded outward on its heavy hinges. It faced the first F-S. In the domed control compartment of the other craft he saw Curly and Jack Horner.

They had slammed open one of their ports and were pumping steel into the mass of Black soldiers milling wildly about. The Blacks had gone completely berserk. They were trying to climb up the deck sides of both craft—and Curly and Jack Horner were grimly picking them off like flies. Only a few of the Blacks made any attempt to return the fire. And even then most of their shots found their marks in the bodies of their comrades.

"The hell with them! Get off!"

Dusty's roaring command was spontaneous, and it was instantly drowned out by the crash of gunfire. But as he shouted he reached out and hauled shut the opened section of window. He saw water-tight locking strips, but he made no effort to twist them into place. If he took the damn thing south he'd go by air, not by water.

The instant the dome port was shut, he leaped forward and dropped into a bucket seat just back of a big control board. The Diesel instruments and controls he recognized in one sweeping glance.

Snapping out one free hand, he grabbed the throttle. With the other he grabbed the control stick. And with his left foot he kicked off the wheel brake release.

Jerking his head around he snapped a glance at the other craft, shouted with joy. Curly and Jack had also sealed their compartment and they were rolling forward, Black soldiers still clinging to it in a madman's effort to hold it back.

A grin on his powder-streaked face, Dusty turned forward and started to open the throttle, but hesitated the fraction of a second as wild alarm shot through him. The bomber was already in the air, and racing toward low-hanging clouds. That brought a curse to his lips. But what made him bellow with rage was the second thing he saw.

The F-S on his right was rolling out onto the field. Its props were spinning discs of glistening light, and crouched down in the domed control room were the figures of two Blacks.

All three flying subs taking off; two of them controlled by

Yanks, the third still controlled by Blacks, who were racing off to assist their supreme commander in his flight to Europe.

"Like hell you will!" roared Dusty.

And with that he slammed the throttle wide open, kicked right rudder and sent his own craft swerving crazily around and headed straight for the other F-S!

## CHAPTER 14
## VULTURE STAMPEDE

A SUICIDE effort? Perhaps! But Dusty didn't think of that as he cursed his craft forward. He thought only of preventing that Black-controlled flying sub from leaving the ground.

There was no time to try and figure out how to shoot at the craft. Besides it was armor-plated and undoubtedly immune to anything but the Tetalyne-gas torpedoes. And how they were fired and controlled, he didn't know—and it was no time to stop and find out.

Just one way open—smack into it before it could get up enough speed to leave the ground! Slam into it, lock wings and cripple it hopelessly.

Maybe the Tetalyne torpedoes would blow both craft sky high. Maybe not—maybe their war heads had not been set. Sheer impact did not explode Tetalyne. The timed electric sparker in the war head did that—that, or else the heat of fire.

Crazy, disconnected thoughts racing around in his head, Dusty hunched over the controls and kept his eyes glued to the

THE GUN IN HIS GRIP POUNDED OUT
SOUND AND FLAME.

craft running across his line of travel. The distance between them was less than fifty yards. He shoved the stick forward, sensed the tail coming up and kicked hard on right rudder. A sleek V-shaped wing loomed up directly in front of him. It glistened, almost ominously. Beyond it, behind heavy glass plating, he caught a flash glance of two cruel-featured but startled faces. And then there was a terrific impact, and the dull crunch of metal biting into metal.

Everything began to spin. His body left the bucket seat; was slammed up against the big instrument board, and then slammed back down onto the floor.

He felt as though he were being cartwheeled around inside a whirling barrel. Lights and shadows mingled, separated and mingled again. There was the rasping, half screaming sound of metal being ripped to shreds. There was also the ungodly wail of crumpled props thrashing the air at maximum revs, and slashing at metal shreds.

Above him it seemed very dark. In a crazy abstract way he realized that his craft was flat on its back, yet slightly tipped to one side, due to the domed control room. He was sprawled out on the inside of the glass and gaping dumbly through it at churned-up ground. Instruments that had been wrenched loose were falling down on top of him.

In that bedlam of hell he was unable to move. At the very next second he expected to hear the world-crashing roar of Tetalyne torpedoes letting go, and to fly out into the catharsis that is death.

Sound smashed and beat against his eardrums. It was like

scores of hammers pounding right into his brain, and all the time the ground itself was heaving up and down like the waves of a storm-lashed sea.

The effect made his head swim, made it impossible for him to grab hold of anything for support. Projections within reach seemed to shake free of his hands as he reached for them.

And then suddenly, there was a grinding howl and the terrific vibration stopped. It took him a couple of moments to realize the reason.

The bent and twisted props churning, slashing into crumpled metal had at last jammed against something that would not give to their whirling force, and as a result the pounding powerful tandem Diesels had gone dead.

But though the vibration ceased, the thunder of sound continued. It was a conglomerate roar of a thousand different tones. Dull, crashing thunder, and mingled in with it all was the snarling staccato cracking of machine-gun fire. It was the sound of the last that jerked him out of his befuddled trance. Machine guns were yammering somewhere.

He rolled over on his stomach, got up on his hands and knees. Wasting a few moments, he tried to shove open one of the dome ports, but the weight of the massive craft was crushing the dome into the ground, and he couldn't budge a single section. Pulling himself up on his feet, he stepped up on a corner of the inverted instrument panel, and by flinging up both hands he was able to hook his finger over the lip of the top step leading to the center passageway.

The absurd humor of it brought a crooked grin to his lips.

The craft was on its back, so the steps that normally led down to the center passageway, were now leading up to it, and the floor of the passageway was now the ceiling.

Monkey-like he pulled his body up hand over hand, kicking out to both sides with his feet for bracing. Eventually he wiggled over onto the ceiling of the passageway, scrambled aft, and then went up the lower flight of stamped-out steps.

But when he was still a dozen feet from the locked, up-side-down door near the tail, there was a terrific crash of sound outside. The F-S heaved up into the air and twisted over more on its side.

Unable to brace himself in time, Dusty went slamming up against steel plating with such terrific force that every drop of breath was smashed out of his lungs, and every bone in his body seemed crushed to a pulp.

Choking, coughing, gasping he lay wedged down in the corner groove formed by the wall meeting the ceiling. If it had meant his life, meant everything in fact, he could not have moved. From head to toe he was paralyzed with pain.

FIVE MINUTES, a year, or a century? He had no idea how long he lay wedged in the steel corner. He only became conscious of the fact that his body was in motion again when his head bumped into the heavy sealed door.

Balls of colored light spinning around before his eyes, he fumbled for the sealing lock bolt, and seemed to touch everything else but it. Finally, though, his fingers closed over it. A choked grunt burst from his lips as he braced himself and tugged.

Three times he tugged at it with every ounce of his remaining strength. And on the third tug, it slapped back free. Straightening up he put his shoulder against the door and heaved.

The heavy metal door groaned, swung up a couple of inches, and then dropped down shut as Dusty's strength spent itself. He crouched, fighting for breath for a moment. But as there came another thunderous boom of sound and the ground heaved like a tidal wave, he hurled himself into frenzied action.

Like a human battering ram he heaved up against the door. It groaned again and swung open a foot or so. The momentum of his mad heave carried the upper part of his body up through, and before the heavy door could drop back and crush him across the chest he had slammed the palms of his hands against it, and given it a second mighty shove.

That shove was just enough. The door swung past the vertical and slammed down against the steel side of the craft. A moment later Dusty was entirely through the opening, and a huddled gasping heap on solid ground.

By now everything was an even greater blur of spinning lights and shadows, and rolling, roaring sound. With an effort that was practically automatic, he stumbled up on his feet. Before him was a mountain of twisted and gouged metal. The right wing of his craft had been completely sheared off, and was bent double over the body of the other craft whose tail was tilted at right angles toward the sky.

The sky!

In that moment the truth crashed home. The overcast sky was now a whirling mass of wings—Black wings and Yank wings. Hundreds of planes! Giant bombers, observation crates, sleek pursuit jobs—all twisting, turning, hurtling about in a weird maze of criss-cross jetting streamers of flame.

The bombers! Faber's message had got through.

Dusty laughed wildly as a Black plane suddenly burst into flames and went whirling down. A split-second later, though, the laugh died on his lips.

From the other side of the two crashed flying subs came hoarse shouts, and almost instantly two figures clutching flame-spitting guns came charging toward him.

That he had dropped he knew only when his body hit the ground. That he was returning the fire, he knew only when the gun in his right hand jumped. And that his life had been spared again, he knew only when he saw the two Blacks pitch forward on their faces and lay still.

He lunged forward and tore a small portable machine gun from the lifeless fingers of the nearest Black. Dropping down on one knee he swung the gun around and pulled the trigger at Black blurs racing crazily across the field.

Blacks threw up their hands and dropped like ten-pins. Some of them were actually knocked sidewise, while others seemed to sink down like melted snowmen. Only when the last slug ripped out and the gun was empty did Dusty stop.

Throwing it away, he started to duck down behind a big strip of torn metal, when suddenly he caught sight of an F-S in the air. It was sweeping down through the maze of twisting ships, straight for the center of the field.

He rushed out into the clear, waving his arms wildly at the ship slanting down.

"Beat it!" he bellowed. "Clear out—never mind me—get that thing back home, you fools!"

He couldn't even hear the sound of his own voice. Bombers aloft were starting to shower down their death charges upon the river-front town of Bersimis, about a mile away.

Great fountains of earth and flame spouted into the air, and the ground shook and rocked from the concussion. Black soldiers were racing screaming for their lives toward the far side of the field, away from the circling Yank bombers.

But all that, Dusty didn't even notice. Completely exposed to any marksman who wished to use him as a target, he stood waving at the gliding F-S, making frantic motions to Curly and Jack Horner to leave him and fly the craft away to safety before it was destroyed by the terrible hell raining down from the sky.

Down it came, however, touched ground and rolled to within fifty yards of him. He saw Jack Horner disappear from the domed control room. Split seconds later the tail door opened and the Intelligence man leaped out.

**DUSTY WAS** already racing toward the craft, and he met young Horner about fifteen feet from it. At that moment a bomb struck on the far side of the field. The earth rocked out from under their feet, and they both went sprawling. As though he was almost used to it, Dusty scrambled up, grabbed young Horner and pulled him up.

"You shouldn't have landed!" he roared. "You had a job to do! The bomber with Fire-Eyes—"

"Shut up!" young Horner shouted. "Get in quick, you damn fool—think we were going to leave you—after what you did?"

Dusty didn't bother to answer. All hell breaking loose had drowned out half of the Intelligence man's words. Together they scrambled in through the door, slammed it shut.

"Off, Curly!" shouted Dusty running toward the steps. "Get it off—quick!"

The plane was already in motion by the time he climbed up into the domed compartment. But at that instant a new and entirely different fear gripped him. The bandage was gone from Curly's head, and blood was streaming down the side of his white face.

His lower lip was clenched between his teeth, and his hands gripping the controls were white at the knuckles.

One glance and Dusty realized that Curly's last ounce of strength had fled him. The lean pilot could no longer keep control of the craft. Savage will-power was commanding, but the flesh was too weak. The terrific beating Brooks had taken since his capture was coming to the surface in one last rush.

Dusty was in the act of leaping across the compartment, just as Curly's hands fell from the controls and he went toppling out of the seat. The next second was the longest second in Dusty's whole life.

He thought that he would never get his hands on the controls. The plane was less than a hundred feet off the ground, and it had fallen over on wing and was slicing downward.

He couldn't make it—they were going to hit—smack right

down to join the two other crumpled F-Ss that were being showered with dirt and debris. He'd never make it—

And then somehow he managed to fall into the seat. His groping hands found the controls, and his feet thumped down on the rudder pedals. He held his breath, jumped on the opposite rudder and slammed the stick all the way over. One infinitesimal flicker of time, and then the craft righted itself and went zooming up, hardly five feet from the ground.

Agent 10 was pounding against his bullet-grazed shoulder, shouting like a veritable madman.

"To the left—to the left, Dusty! We can get the ammo storehouses with a torpedo. Our bombers have already smashed the factory. To the left—head straight for them!"

Instantly Dusty swung the big craft around, absently realizing that it was sluggish on the controls. It practically lumbered around, settled on a dead-on course for a squared area of twenty-five or thirty low-roofed stone buildings in the distance.

"Hold her steady, Dusty!"

As Agent 10 yelled the words he moved toward a side panel covered with instruments and Black Invader inscriptions. He swung down a lever, twisted a rheostat, and snapped a switch. Then he reached for a trigger fixed to the wall. With the other hand he slipped a set of radio phones over his head.

A second later he pulled the trigger. Dusty felt the ship give a sort of lurch; thought he saw something streak out from under the nose. Out the corner of his eye he could see Jack Horner twisting the short-wave dial this way and that. And then suddenly he took his hand off the dial, leaned forward and peered ahead.

Dusty was no longer looking at him. His eyes were also clamped on the squared area of buildings ahead. It seemed years, and then without warning, a great ocean of rolling gray clouds appeared in the air just off the roofs of the buildings.

They became completely hidden from view. And then a solid sheet of red flame leaped high into the sky, and where the rolling smoke clouds had been was the seething orange of yellow flame. It was as though the very air itself was on fire.

One great flash, and before it winked out a second and a third flash spewed upward from a swirling, whirling vortex of seething hell. The instant they appeared Dusty instinctively leaned every ounce of his weight against the controls, veered the giant craft away from the flaming tongues that seemed to be virtually reaching out as though to pull it into their midst, and poked its nose up for the clouds.

For hellish moments he feared that Jack Horner had fired the aerial torpedo too late; that they would be slammed down out of the air by the very fury of the thundering hell it created.

The F-S seemed to lose altitude, rather than gain it. The raging inferno just ahead and below had become invisible quicksand that was sucking them down into it. The air all about them was tinged with crimson. Shadows raced by, invisible hammers pounded against the side of the craft, and with each passing second they seemed to be sinking lower and lower— being sucked down into that boiling chaos.

And then, when it seemed that all was lost, that they were

to be destroyed by their own folly, the F-S took on a sudden change of life. Its spinning props seemed to "dig" into the air, and the craft went soaring upwards.

"God—thought we were gone!"

Jack Horner's choking cry of relief came to Dusty's ears as almost a whisper. He was too occupied with keeping the craft thundering upward. And a moment later a flight of Yank wings dropped down upon them. Jetting flame cut across the heavens and steel slugs hammered against the sides of the F-S.

And it wasn't until that moment that Dusty realized that there was no way for the Yank planes in the air to know that the one he flew was Yank-controlled. Even as the thought came to him he shot out his free hand, snapped on radio contact, and spun the wave-length dial to S.O.S. Emergency reading.

"All Yank planes!" he roared into the transmitter tube. "Don't fire on Flying Submarine. We are Yanks! This is Ayres speaking. Don't fire on F-S!"

HE REPEATED the message three times before Yank planes closing in, stopped their fire and pulled away. But Black pilots had heard his message also, and they came tearing down like so many metal vultures.

It seemed as though hundreds of them had suddenly appeared out of nowhere.

The sides of the F-S clattered as burst after burst of steel death whipped against it. One of the left dome windows cracked in a thousand different places, and a second later a whirlwind of hell blasted right through it and Dusty felt as though his left arm had been torn from his body.

He looked down and saw that it still was there. A strip of heavy window bracing had been chewed off by the savage burst of fire, and had slammed it against his arm. But the control board for the aerial torpedo was a splintered shambles. Had the burst arrived two seconds before it would have buried itself in Agent 10's skull. By a miracle he had flung himself to the floor, and now he was crouched there as splintered glass and broken instruments showered down on top of him.

A few feet from him Curly Brooks sat half propped against the wall, a dazed, foggy look in his blue eyes. Weakly he was fumbling with one hand at the reopened gash on his temple.

A flash look was all that Dusty could take, and then he hurled himself into action. There were double trigger trips on the control stick. Where the guns were mounted, he did not know. He simply jabbed the trigger trips forward. Instantly the nose of the craft spewed out twin streams of jetting flame from guns perfectly streamlined into the body.

He let out a yell of wild joy. To jab trigger trips and hear guns yammering at his touch brushed the cobwebs from his brain. To hell with trick radio-controlled torpedoes. Here was something he could handle with the best of them. And with that he went to work in the very center of a spinning, darting hell.

A Black cabin observation plane, streaked past his nose. He thumped down on rudder, swung the F-S and fired. He missed by a mile, pulled the nose up, and sent hot steel piling through cabin windows. The last he saw of the plane it was falling into a wild power spin.

He didn't give it a second look. A big Black bomber was

coming in from the right. He hauled the F-S around charged at it and blasted away with both guns. The bomber tried to veer away, but as it did four Yank pursuit planes came thundering down from above, and the Black bomber pilot probably died not even knowing what had hit him.

What happened from then on was not a series of individual events to Dusty. It was all one great conglomeration of jumbled up action. He had glimpses of planes hurtling earthward in flames—some of them going down as a result of his own marksmanship.

He had glimpses of raging oceans of flame below, that completely engulfed the town of Bersimis for miles around—the St. Lawrence, itself, seemed to be a river of fire. He never saw the F-S drome again. It was nothing but churned up ground, spouting flame and smoke. He knew that two more of the dome windows had been blasted to bits by flying steel. He knew that everything in the compartment about him was a bullet-riddled shambles, practically.

And then after an eternity of whirling chaos, he became conscious of Agent 10's voice screaming in his ear.

"Enough, Dusty! Enough—we've done plenty—the others have them on the run! Pull out—let's get this thing back home!"

**IT WAS** like being shaken out of a crazy nightmare. Blood-red haze cleared from Dusty's eyes, and he realized that he was leading a tornado of American planes thundering after a beaten horde of Black vultures. Yeah, Jack was right—better get this damn thing down to the States while he was still conscious. God, but he hurt all over.

173

But as a sudden thought struck him he jerked up straight.

"Fire-Eyes!" he yelled to Jack Horner. "Did he—"

He stopped short. The Intelligence man was shrugging and shaking his head.

"I don't know," he said. "The bomber was in the clouds before Curly could get us off. That F-S you smacked was trying to block us off. If it hadn't been for you—"

"You mean he was going for this crate?" Dusty burst out.

The other nodded.

"Hell yes!" he said. "They'd even opened fire on us. He realized what you were up to too late. God, I thought you'd been killed. Curly cleared the wreck of both ships by less than a dozen feet.

"If you hadn't plowed into him it would have been curtains for all of us. I thought you were a crazy fool—going for that second ship. But it's funny—it was that crazy action of yours that saved the whole thing."

Dusty nodded absently, turned and glanced back at Curly. The lean pilot was still slumped against the side wall, but there was less of a dazed look in his eyes. In fact he grinned weakly as his eyes met Dusty's.

"To think I'd ever have to let you take over, because I couldn't hang on!" he mumbled. "God, am I getting lousy!"

Dusty grinned, and a song was in his heart. When Curly could wise-crack he was a hell of a long ways from death's door. Swinging the F-S around he headed south, and let a squadron of Yank planes drop into escort position. He was tired as hell. His whole body ached and burned. But a new and even fiercer sort of strength was beginning to flow through his body, and he knew that he could fly the damn F-S twice around the world without passing out.

"Yeah," he grunted at Jack Horner. "It's funny—the funniest, damnedest mix-up we've hit so far. Even now, it all seems too cockeyed to make sense. But, in a way, the Blacks licked themselves. And if that rat, Fire-Eyes, has slipped through our patrol planes and is safely on his way to Europe, he probably realizes it more than we do."

Jack Horner gave him a frowning look.

"What do you mean, they licked themselves?" he grunted.

"No co-operation," Dusty replied. "Ekar and that double of mine. If they'd worked together we would have been out of luck right at the start. But they didn't. For some reason, jealousy, I guess, they hated each other—tried to shoot the works single handed.

"Neither knew what the other was doing, and that helped us trip them both. Say, by the way, you didn't tell me—how the hell did you live through that crash when the F-S rammed our patrol boat?"

Agent 10 absently wiped dripping sweat from his face.

"Don't know," he said. "I remember being thrown clear of the boat. And I have a faint memory of floating around, and hanging onto a broken locker board, or maybe it was the cockpit seat. Anyway, the next thing I knew definitely, I was on the shore and some Black soldiers were pumping water out of me.

"When I could talk I gave them a cock and bull story—even got them to drive me into Bersimis. From there, I made my way to the field. You see they spoke about the F-Ss—said that was what hit the patrol boat. If either you or Curly were alive I had a hunch that's where you would be—at the field. Just luck all around. God help us, if the streak ever breaks."

"It hasn't yet," Dusty said grimly. "And somehow I don't think it ever will. Hope not, anyway. At least I hope it sticks with me until I've squared myself with that cockeyed Northeastern Area Staff. And you too, Jack! We're—"

"Don't worry about Northeastern Staff!" snorted Agent 10 wrathfully. "When they learn what happened today—how you made it possible for this F-S to be delivered into American hands for examination and copying, they'll vote you a string of medals a mile long."

"No they won't," said Dusty. "I flub-dubbed so many things that I really rate a kick in the pants. Two men made all this possible. To their memory goes all the credit, every bit. And to their families, everlasting help and assistance from the Government. Those two members of your department, Jack—Travis and Faber. What we did, kid, wasn't a damn thing compared to what they accomplished, and paid for."

Jack Horner nodded soberly.

"Right!" he said grimly. "It's men with their courage and eternal fighting spirit, who will finally smash these damn Blacks back into the hell where they belong!"

Neither spoke for a moment or two. As a matter of fact it was Curly who broke the silence.

"Hey! A little more speed! I'm hungry, and I need a drink bad!"

Dusty turned around and grinned at his pal, who was now fully conscious, but much too weak from the loss of blood to trouble moving up closer to them. Then he caught Agent 10's eye, winked.

"Hell, Jack, he's been listening! Now I suppose he'll be wanting to take the little credit that we deserve, away from us. I'll bet he tells the newspapers that he—"

"Never did like flying with slow-motion pilots!" Curly cut in wrathfully. "Snap it up—action—get some speed out of this thing! I'm telling you I need that drink bad. A couple of them, in fact!"

POPULAR PUBLICATIONS
# HERO PULPS

LOOK FOR MORE SOON!

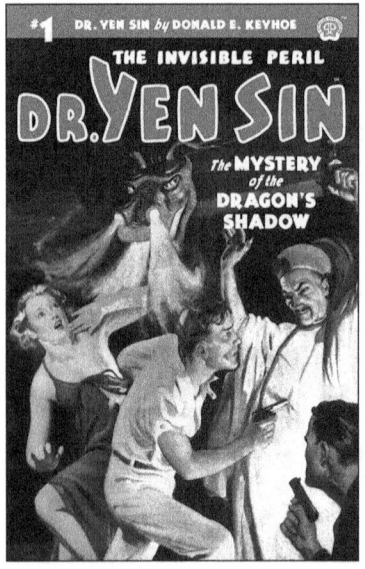

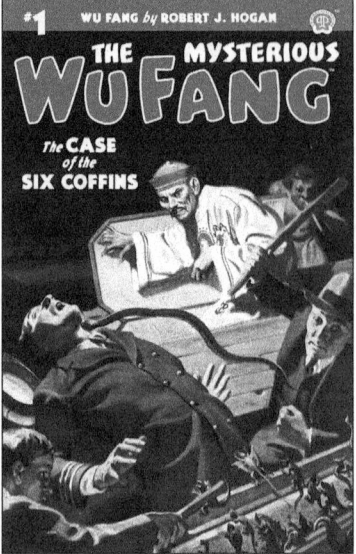

# ALTUS PRESS · THE NAME IN PULP PUBLICATIONS

Available at AltusPress.com and better bookstores.